Enchanting Blend

A PARAMOUR BAY MYSTERY
BOOK THREE

KENNEDY LAYNE

KENNEDY LAYNE PUBLISHING, INC.

Dedication

Jeffrey & Cole — I love you!

About the Book

Shenanigans are brewing up once more in Paramour Bay as USA Today Bestselling Author Kennedy Layne continues her cozy paranormal mystery series...

New Year's Eve is just a week away, and Raven Marigold knows exactly how she wants to spend the remainder of her holiday break before the glittery ball drops—solving a fifty-three-year-old murder and clearing her grandmother's reputation!

Raven doesn't have a lot of time between memorizing enchanting spells, creating magical tea blends, and finally going out on her first date in months, but she's willing to combine all three if it means eliminating the shadow of guilt that has loomed over her family's surname for over five decades.

Grab your pointy party hats, bring your mystical noisemakers, and ring in the New Year with the quirky characters of Paramour Bay!

One

"IS that who I think it is?"

My best friend's meddlesome inquiry captured my attention immediately. Heidi always had this tone of excitement when something big was about to happen, and today's alert was no exception to the rule.

"Who?" I peered over the edge of the counter as I attempted to look around the cash register. All I could see from my vantage point was the twinkling Christmas lights outlining the glass door. The generally accepted time to take them down was only a few days away, so I wouldn't buck the system. I would wait until the day after the new year to store them until the next holiday season. "I can't see anyone from here."

"I'm pretty sure you're about to get an unexpected visitor."

"Then hurry and flip the open sign to closed," I retorted, going back to my task at hand. "I finally have a long weekend ahead of me, a date that is obviously way overdue, and an oddly worded enchantment to conquer. Who would have thought taming eyebrows required an entirely different spell than the hair growth remedy I created for Candy over at the salon?"

1

I restocked the last of the brown paper bags I used for my customer's purchases, pleased with the frayed edges that gave the different-sized shopping sacks an antiquated appearance that my grandmother would have liked. The fact that the print distributor had added *Tea, Leaves, & Eves* in a scripted font was just icing on the cake for me.

The entire day had pretty much been spent getting the tea shop ready for the start of the new year. New Year's Eve was on Monday, and I wanted a fresh beginning with the upcoming year. If the holiday weekend ahead was any indication, the following three hundred and sixty-five days were going to be even better.

A flurry of butterflies had set up residence in my stomach at the thought of my first date with Sheriff Liam Drake. There was something about the man's character that left me breathless. We were supposed to have gone to dinner a few weeks ago, but our initial plans got sidetracked when his sister surprised him with a visit for the duration of the holidays.

"Heidi?" It took me a minute to realize she hadn't moved toward the front door. "Did you—"

Heidi's hand came out of nowhere to land on top of my head the moment the glass door to the shop activated the golden bell. She quickly pushed me back down and shifted closer, not caring that I barely caught myself from tumbling off my lowly stool to the floor.

"Mrs. Barnes, what a pleasant surprise," Heidi called out, though her greeting wasn't sincere in the least. Trust me, her reaction was warranted. I even had to stifle a groan of irritation at the thought of the woman's arrival myself. "What can I do for you today?"

My knees were beginning to ache the longer I stayed in this position, but I was afraid I'd alert Cora to my hidden location below the counter if I so much as stretched my legs. The last thing I wanted to do was have Cora Barnes figure out that I was hiding from her behind the cash register.

"I was hoping to speak with Raven," Cora announced, the haughtiness in her tone impossible to miss even with my clenched teeth. I rolled my eyes, not having to hide the fact that I was annoyed at this development. I didn't get a lot of 'me' time as a relatively new small business owner, and Cora was one of the few residents in town who hadn't exactly welcomed me with open arms. "Is she in the back room? I know that she hasn't left the shop for the holiday weekend."

Dang it.

Busted.

Heidi looked down at me in chagrin and gave me a small shrug. Well, she'd tried her best. The loyalty of a best friend was priceless.

"Hi, Cora." I had shifted on my black knee-high boots and popped up from my hiding spot with a smile on my face, attempting to act as if hiding behind the counter was the most natural proposition. My grin might have grown a smidgen when the older woman startled a bit, but I did try and curb my satisfaction at giving her a start. The last thing I needed to do was have bad karma on my heels when my life was finally getting on track. "We were just about to close up the shop and close out the receipts on this year's accounts. Was there something you needed?"

"I was hoping to speak with you privately." Cora slid a squinted glance in Heidi's direction along with a forced smile, but there was no way I was going to be in the company of a woman who disliked my family without the aid of my BFF. Okay, dislike might have been too generous of a verb. I was pretty sure I'd seen fire coming out of her facial orifices the last time she and my mother had been in the same room. I had almost called the fire department out of desperation. "There's something I need to say that's long overdue."

To say it was tempting to hear Cora's reason for seeking me out was an understatement. I came very close to asking Heidi to go into the back room that I used as a storage area to appease the woman, but I wasn't that crazy.

"There's nothing you can't say to me in front of Heidi," I informed Cora, resting my hands on the counter. I had a pretty good inkling of what she wanted to discuss with me. Did she have to show up here and rub the guilt in my face? "This is about the Secret Santa gift exchange, isn't it? I didn't know that Monty was allergic to peanuts. No one told me. I've already apologized profusely to him, and I'll make sure that I don't include that type of tea blend in an anonymous gift exchange ever again."

Monty was an older gentleman who owned the hardware store, and he'd participated in the Christmas party that the shop owners in town had thrown last weekend. The get-together had given me an opportunity to get to know the other residents, but having an ambulance called to the festivities hadn't exactly been in the cards.

I'd learned a very valuable lesson that night—never compile a tea gift basket without keeping the labels on the tea bags.

Monty loved his tea, so it hadn't struck me as odd when he'd asked the bartender at the tavern for a cup of hot water after he'd opened his present. It wasn't like everyone didn't know the gift was from me. *Tea, Leaves, & Eves* had been delicately hand-painted on the porcelain tea mug.

Unfortunately, it wasn't long afterward that Monty broke out into red hives and his face began to change to a color that one could easily recognize as purple.

I thought for sure I was going to be responsible for the man's peanut oil-induced death.

"This is...personal," Cora declared, clasping her gloved hands behind her back as if she were facing off with an adversary prior to a duel.

Personal?

Oh, this couldn't be good at all.

What had my mother done now?

I was tempted to tell Cora to turn back around on those expensive brown winter boots of hers, but I managed to refrain myself from lashing out. You see, my mother and Cora have a history of bad blood between them. The feud started way before I was born, but I guess I should introduce myself before I give away any more of their backstory.

My past is a bit complicated, and I wouldn't want you to be lost in the story.

My name is Raven Lattice Marigold, and it's a pleasure to meet you.

Around two and a half months ago, I discovered some things about myself that might surprise you. It certainly did me. Or maybe not, if the blurb of this particular tale caught your interest.

Anyway, I come from a long line of witches.

That's right—the magical kind.

Witches.

It took me some time to adjust to the news myself, but I've come to embrace my newfound powers. I mean, who wouldn't want to be a witch capable of casting magical spells?

Honestly, I still get rather giddy just thinking about it.

My unexpected gift came along with my Nan's familiar. I'd introduce you to him, but Leo left around lunchtime and hasn't reappeared for some reason or another. I should warn you that he can be rather snarky and downright rude at times, but he'll grow on you. Of that, I'm certain.

I actually have a soft spot for Leo after all he's been through, but I'll catch you up on his history later. It's a bit more complicated than my accidental tale.

Anyway, no one in the small town of Paramour Bay, Connecticut is aware that the Marigolds are actual bona fide witches. I've been told it's one of the coven's rules, not that I've ever personally met another witch from outside the family. I've been trying not to take offense at what must certainly be a snub of some sort, but I'm pretty sure it has to do with the fact that I'm new to this whole supernatural thing.

Either that or someone discovered that I'd broken the sacred rule by telling Heidi the truth about my family's history. I wasn't normally a rule breaker, but I was definitely a bad liar. Awful, if truth be told.

It was a huge relief to know that I no longer had to keep a secret from my best friend as I tumbled along on this wondrous journey.

All that aside, I'm pretty sure that Cora has a sense that all is not right with the Marigolds. Maybe she sensed the supernatural nature of our family's origins. It could have something to do with my little side business that all started with my grandmother's desire to help the community of Paramour Bay.

You see, Rosemary Lattice Marigold was the original owner of *Tea, Leaves, & Eves*. My grandmother had a pretty successful reputation for dabbling in...are you ready for this? *Herbal* remedies and *holistic* medicines. *Natural* cures for the body. Pretty nifty, huh? I'm sure you noticed the words herbal, holistic, and natural are italicized.

You see, my Nan sprinkled a bit of magic over those particular remedies.

Her success rate was incredible.

To sum it up, Nan used the gift of her ancestors to help others overcome their ills.

I've continued her traditions, with a few minor setbacks. Really, just minor side effects. Nothing to worry about. Learning spells and using my power hasn't been altogether easy, you know. Much to Leo's displeasure, I was a slow learner in the enchantment area. I have had a few successes, though.

Take the former sheriff—Otis Finley. His arthritis was becoming worse and worse until Nan created a tea blend under the guise of an herbal remedy. Within days, Otis was back to fishing and enjoying an occasional night out with his lovely wife. I might have caused Leo's tail to go completely numb for a few hours, but it was one of the first enchanted blends that I was able to create.

It really was just a small hiccup partway through. Nothing too drastic.

As for my most recent visitor, Cora Barnes, she was completely against aging.

Cora had entered her fifties kicking and screaming, and there didn't seem to be an end to what she'd do to keep those wrinkles at bay. I'd swear that she would actually bathe in Earl Gray tea if it meant shedding a few years off her body. Money was no object for her, but I'd cut off her supply of the bewitched Chai tea blend that she'd been getting from Nan due to Cora's temper.

Cora made the mistake of being rude to my mother.

I mentioned before that loyalty was priceless, and I stand by my convictions.

My mom and I might butt heads too often, but she was still my mother.

"Heidi, would you mind grabbing my winter dress coat

from the back room?" I asked, nodding toward my best friend so she'd know that I was okay being alone with Cora.

Maybe I was crazy, after all.

Heidi arched an eyebrow that was just a smidgen darker than her blonde hair. She wasn't known for her tact and tended to speak her mind.

For that matter, so did I.

We were both from New York, and it had taken me a while to get used to the small-town mentality of hospitality before tempest—which meant I mind my manners and accept that anything I said or did could be front page fodder for the local paper.

Hiding the fact that I was a true witch certainly wasn't easy in a population of three hundred and fifty-five residents.

"What is it that you want to talk to me about, Cora?" I'd waited for Heidi to disappear between the strings of magical ivory-colored fairy beads, which screened the storage area from the front of the shop. The melodic clicking soothed my nerves and reminded me that this was my turf. I held the upper hand. I didn't mean that completely in a territorial manner. I was just more confident in my place of business than anywhere else in town, not that I'd have to hide a body later or something like that. "If it's not Monty's peanut allergy, is this about the New Year's Eve party at the wax museum?"

I know what you're thinking.

A wax museum in such a small town?

I'd thought the same thing the first time I'd heard about it, but the odd out-of-place business was still there all the same.

"No, it's about our...relationship."

Relationship?

As in business relationship?

It was a known fact that Cora and her husband, Desmond,

wanted to expand their malt shop. In order to do so, either myself or Molly would have to give up our leases on our stores and move to another spot on the main road—River Bay.

Molly owned the quaint boutique on the other side of the malt shop, and she wasn't about to give up any space when she'd coveted such a great storefront on the town's main thoroughfare. For that matter, neither was I.

"Cora, I thought you'd already heard from Oliver that I renewed my lease for the next three years. I know I can sell the shop in one year, according to Nan's will, but I like Paramour Bay too much to leave." It was almost a relief to know that this was why Cora had come into the tea shop. Anything else might have ruined my upcoming weekend, and I didn't want my anticipation tainted in the slightest. "I know that's not what you wanted to hear, but I—"

"Raven, dear, I'm not here about the storefront issue." Cora somehow managed to straighten her shoulders even more, and that wasn't an easy thing to do considering she was one of those women who had perfect posture. I suddenly had a bad feeling that my long overdue extended weekend wasn't going to work out quite as I had planned. "I'm here to..."

What had she said?

I caught myself leaning over the counter to hear the mumbled word she'd uttered toward the end of her sentence, but I had to have heard it incorrectly.

"I'm here to..."

Once again, I couldn't quite make out what Cora was trying to say.

Her thin red lips seemed to distort in an odd manner every time she tried to finish her statement. The crazy thing about this rather odd conversation was that it was coming across as if she was attempting to apologize.

That would never happen.

Would it?

An unexpected thud came from the back room, telling me that Heidi had knocked something over. She most likely had her ear pressed against the string of ivory-colored fairies, doing her best to hear my exchange with Cora.

Heidi was probably just as surprised as I was.

"Cora?"

I wasn't one to hold grudges, unlike my mother. Now that woman was a pro in the grudge department. A person could seal their fate in an instant with one wrong move. Honestly, it was a wonder she hadn't received some type of medal for her commitment to hoarding years of resentment inside of her conflicted soul.

Did I tell you that my mother gave up witchcraft to have a normal life?

Yep.

Cold turkey.

You're wondering who would do something like that, and I don't blame you.

It's crazy.

Anyhow, Mom and Nan had a falling out about the whole witchcraft thing and me. My mother ended up moving to New York City when she was still pregnant with me. I don't recall a time we ever came back to visit Paramour Bay, and it wasn't until Nan dropped dead of a heart attack on her daily walk that I had even stepped foot over the county line.

I digress.

We were talking about grudges, and I wasn't one to hold onto them like anchors, given the propensity of the other members of my family to do just that. With that said, I don't think I ever expected to be in a situation where Cora would ever ask for my forgiveness.

I was torn on what to say and how to act.

"I'm sorry, Raven."

Wow.

Shock flooded my system like white lightning. The drink, not the bolt.

Cora had finally managed to get the expression of guilt out of her mouth by running her words together. Her relief was evident, and it allowed her to continue.

"Regina and I have never quite seen things eye to eye, and it was wrong of me to assume that you and I should have the same relationship. I'd like to start over, if that's still a possibility."

The right thing for me to do in this astounding moment would be to accept Cora's apology and move on.

I know this.

Our businesses were side by side, the town was too small to avoid one another, and we practically ran into each other on a daily basis.

Yet a part of me didn't want to betray my mother's determined efforts.

Now, wasn't this a tricky situation?

I figured I'd better clarify a thing or two before giving my answer.

"Cora, is this olive branch being offered just to get me to make you the Chai tea blend that helps with the appearance of aging?"

I also wasn't as naïve as I might appear on page.

Living in New York had a way of jading a person's sense of propriety.

Cora was known to manipulate people to get what she

wanted, and I definitely had something she wanted. Fortunately, she believed that the tea blend Nan had concocted for her wrinkles contained antioxidants to slow the aging process.

It was easy to see that I hadn't made any in a while, although Cora was a beautiful woman in her own right. She was the one who had a problem with growing old gracefully.

"I'm not saying our previous arrangement won't be a benefit to our truce, but spending time with certain members of my family this holiday season made me realize that I haven't been fair to you." A bit of color had come back to Cora's cheeks, though that might have been due to the fact that she hadn't taken off her coat since walking through the front door of the tea shop. It was freezing outside, and she probably hadn't expected the apology to take this long. "I'd truly like there to be peace between the two of us."

How do I say yes when I know that she and my mother are still at odds?

"I'd like that, too," I replied honestly, wondering if there was a way to extend this mending of matters between her and my mother. I even held out my hand to seal the deal, not caring that Cora returned my gesture with leather-gloved fingers. Boy, was that material soft or what? It literally felt like it had been dipped in butter. "Cora, I do have to ask—why don't you and my mother get along?"

I might have just ruined my beautiful moment with Cora.

She immediately shifted with unease on those brown boots that probably cost more than my entire ensemble. As soft as those leather gloves were, they might actually be more expensive than my complete wardrobe hanging in my closet.

I should have let bygones be bygones, but I needed to attempt a reconciliation if there was a chance to mend fences between Cora and my mother.

"Looking back, I suppose it all started when rumors were swirling around about the old murder that took place when Regina and I were still in diapers." Cora appeared a bit contrite, which told me more than my mother had seen fit to share with me. Unfortunately, Cora didn't seem willing to offer up an apology to Mom for whatever may have happened between the two of them in the past. "It then spiraled out of control over the years until our group splintered."

"Group?" This was the first I was hearing about other people being involved, but it shouldn't have surprised me. High school was basically a ton of oddball cliques thrown together with gasoline and matches. "Who was in the group?"

In case you're wondering, there was a specific reason I didn't ask about the old murder. I'd already been informed of the only unsolved case in Paramour Bay's history that had occurred fifty-three years ago...which just happened to be the age of my mother. It didn't escape me that Cora and Mom would *not* have been in diapers. Interestingly enough, their mothers would have been pregnant with them at the time the crime had been committed.

"Oh," Cora gave a light, nervous laugh and flicked back her hair. "A lot of our old friends have moved away. You know how it is. Anyway, a few things were said about Rosemary that your mother didn't appreciate. In hindsight, I can understand why. Words can be very hurtful, and none of us realized the damage we were causing at the time. I do regret my part in all of it."

I suppose that was something.

It was probably best I accept her apology and move on.

Right?

Cora hadn't meant to spark my interest in such an old murder, but there's something that I should tell you—I've previously solved two murders.

Who was to say that I couldn't solve this one?

Oh no. No, no, no, no, no.

It looks like you get to meet Leo, after all.

That's Mr. Leo to our readers, Raven.

I'm not sure whether or not I should apologize in advance.

Thankfully, Cora hadn't noticed his sudden presence.

Did I mention that familiars can disappear at will and that witches can literally hear familiars talk inside their heads?

I can't leave you alone for two seconds, can I? Listen here, Miss Nancy Drew. You're done being an amateur sleuth. Done. The last time you decided to use witchcraft to help solve a murder, we were almost discovered by the minions. Oh, and let's not forget that we almost died. You're going to get us both killed if you keep this up.

Leo didn't have the best opinion of the average citizen, but Heidi was slowly changing his mind.

Heidi is special.

Leo is also overly dramatic and hopelessly in love with Heidi.

"Maybe there's hope for you and my mother to reconcile in the future," I told Cora now that I'd gotten Leo off the topic of my current hobby of solving crimes. Who knew I was such an adrenaline junky? "Will I see you at the New Year's Eve party? I heard from Elsie and Wilma that there's even a ball drop of sorts in the grand room of the wax museum."

I walked around the counter to escort Cora to the exit, figuring Heidi was chomping at the bit to discuss this latest development. One thing was for certain—for such a small town, Paramour Bay served as a wealth of gossip and small-town entertainment.

You hid Heidi in the storage room? How could you?

"Desmond and I will be there fashionably late, as usual."

Cora was back in full form now that I'd accepted her olive branch. "That reminds me. I need to pick up my new dress from Justine's shop. She had to hem the waist a bit so that the material rested just so on my hips. I've lost some weight over the holidays."

Do you think she owns a mirror?

"I'm sure you'll look stunning in your gown, Cora," I placated, not knowing what else to say. My figure was okay according to various women's magazines, but I'd certainly gotten my hips from my mother. No amount of fabric could hide my hourglass shape. It was the sole reason I stuck to flowy long skirts. "Make sure you have some type of wrap. This cold weather isn't going anywhere anytime soon, and the museum is usually kept at a cooler than usual temperature due to the wax figures."

I'd heard that last detail from Elsie and Wilma. Those two ladies were a wealth of information when it came to the town's history and current events.

Cora left the shop with a wiggle of her gloved fingers, seemingly very satisfied with how her visit had turned out. Her small smile made me wary, but I couldn't worry about what she could or couldn't do to my reputation.

As long as she was kept in the dark about me being a witch, all was right with my world.

Not if you go digging around in that old murder.

"I can't believe that old bat just apologized!" Heidi came out of the back room with our coats, the suitcase she'd brought with her for the weekend visit, and a big smile on her face. She'd inadvertently interrupted what was sure to be one of Leo's infamous lectures. It didn't matter. I had my best friend for the next four days, and we were going to move mountains and empty a few wine bottles. "I should have recorded this epic moment. Did Cora have any crow left in the corners of her mouth or did you fold by handing her a napkin?"

"Don't be so mean," I warned, still not wanting to invite karma into our lives. Just in case, I flipped the hanging sign on the door to closed. Hopefully, it would keep the evil spirits at bay. "It takes a big person to admit when they've been wrong. Cora didn't exactly welcome me to town with open arms, and now I know why."

"What is Leo carrying on about now?" Heidi asked with a frown of concern. She dropped our jackets on the counter before walking over to the display window. I mentioned before that witches could hear familiars, but Leo's words were just a mass of jumbled meows to Heidi. He'd succeeded in his devious plan, though—to have Heidi fawn all over him. "Raven, what did you do to him this time?"

I shot Leo an annoyed glance when Heidi gently picked him up and held him against her chest, even rubbing her hand up and down his scruffy orange and black fur. The story I'd chosen to tell the townsfolk was that Leo was a rescue I'd taken in off the streets. There was no other way to explain his...well, his rather disheveled appearance.

Tell the readers why. Go ahead. There's nothing you can say that won't have them imagining me on the cover of GQ. *Those models all have scruffy beards, too.*

Leo practically purred those words as Heidi continued to shower him with adoration. I was actually grateful they'd made it to this place in their relationship, because Heidi's initial reaction to the supernatural hadn't gone over as well as I'd originally expected.

"Aren't you just a handsome kitty?" Heidi crooned, planting smooches on the top of Leo's head.

Leo's left eye, which was freakishly larger than his right,

gradually closed as he soaked in her affection like a sponge. That wasn't the only odd feature on his rather plumpish body. His whiskers were bent every which way—no pun intended there—and the crink in his tail would make anyone wince, for sure.

Oh, and Leo has a short-term memory loss disorder that can be truly frustrating at certain times.

And I blame your grandmother for all of it.

I couldn't argue with Leo on that point, because Nan had dabbled in black magic to unnaturally extend his life here on earth to help me adjust to my new life.

I should be very thankful, because goodness knows that my mother certainly wasn't helping me out in that department. It was like pulling teeth to get my mother to visit me here in Paramour Bay. She'd wanted nothing to do with my apprenticeship into witchcraft.

Looking back over my time here in this quaint little town, I realized that there was a handful of residents who still spoke to me with caution. There might be a few who suspected something was out of sorts.

I'm pretty sure I've figured out the reason why.

No, you haven't.

"Heidi, our weekend plans have changed," I declared, becoming rather excited at the prospect of clearing my grandmother's name. It was long overdue. Maybe, just maybe, I could clear the shadow of doubt that has been hanging over the Marigold surname and allow Regina Lattice Marigold to return home to her roots. I did want to clarify one thing before we began this mini-adventure. "My date for the New Year's Eve bash hasn't changed, but everything else has."

Nothing has changed. Please, for the love of catnip, don't go digging up the past.

Leo had become agitated to the point that Heidi had to set him down in between the cash register and our coats. She shot me an exasperated glance that told me I shouldn't upset him, but she didn't constantly have to hear his incessant complaining about humans.

I don't complain. I state the facts. And right now, you're causing my blood pressure and my anxiety level to rise significantly. I believe I'm in need of more catnip. Where's my pipe?

"You do complain," I countered with an unapologetic smile. I refused to allow Leo's bad mood to ruin my festive spirit. Now that I'd made the decision to look into the fifty-three-year-old murder that had cast a pallor on my surname, nothing was going to burst my bubble. "But you're stuck with me, and I'm stuck with you. We have to make the most of it, Leo."

Okay. Forget a few puffs of catnip. You wouldn't understand the need for it, anyway. But for the love of all things supernatural, cancel your date with the good ol' sheriff and leave the past buried where it belongs. As in, dead buried...under six feet of dirt.

"No can do, Leo." I was going to start the year off right, and hopefully, that included a kiss from one very handsome sheriff. I walked back around the counter to where I'd stored my purse. "Heidi, are you up for an adventure?"

She gasped and shook her head in mock disapproval.

"I thought you knew me, Raven." Heidi grabbed her coat and small suitcase. She stopped halfway to the door, looking back over her shoulder in question. That's right. I tend to forget that she couldn't hear my entertaining conversations with Leo. "What exactly are we getting up to this weekend?"

"We, my dear friend, are going to solve a fifty-three-year-old murder."

Two

"LIAM?"

I'd expected the police station to be silent without the dispatcher, Eileen, sitting behind her desk, but there was soft seasonal music drifting from the overhead speakers. A small decorated tree from this past week's holiday sat on a corner table adorned with tinsel, various handcrafted ornaments, and colorful lights. A bright silver star completed the ensemble.

The station was still decked out with oversized red and green bulbs hanging from the ceiling, thick garland strewn around the few desks that had been positioned in the large open area, and topped off with a red and white wreath hanging from the sheriff's private office door.

I didn't want to alarm Liam with my sudden appearance, so I called out to him again.

Why wasn't he answering?

There was a golden hue shining out into the main area of the police station from his office, but I couldn't see his desk from where I was standing.

I waited for the palm of my hand to grow warmer than

usual, considering I had my gloves on. They weren't nearly as nice as Cora's leather ones, but I really loved the emerald-green color of the imitation material.

In case you're wondering what I meant about heat in the palm of my hand, it appeared that my powers came from an energy force derived from nature.

I know...pretty cool, huh?

This amazing ability allowed me to sense when something wasn't quite right or when the balance was askew, but my skin wasn't tingling.

Maybe Liam had gone to the restroom. A quick glance in that direction revealed a darkened room with the door left ajar. Nope. He wasn't in there. I swung my gaze back to his personal domain.

I'd watched enough horror flicks to know that this is where something would happen if a killer was on the loose. Good thing I was investigating a murder that had taken place over fifty-three years ago and not today.

Chances were pretty good I could outrun the perpetrator if he was still alive.

"Hello?"

The radio station suddenly switched to playing a carol with an up-tempo beat, which was preferable to the slower one that was rather melancholy...and a bit foreboding now that Christmas was over. It didn't surprise me that Eileen was still playing holiday music. She had a major obsession with Christmas. At least, if the gaudy sweaters she'd worn for the past month were anything to go by. Her larger-than-life holiday clothing collection must require its own closet during the off-season.

I can still hear those gold bells sewn onto the fabric from a mile away.

I almost tripped over my long skirt spinning around thanks to Leo's unexpected presence.

"Go away," I warned with a whisper. I couldn't see him anywhere. Leo was pulling one of those tricks where he baited me into looking foolish in front of Liam. "I'm serious. Go bother Heidi. She's warming up the car."

And leave you to fend for yourself? I don't think so. We'll both end up in jail.

"Raven?"

I swung back around at the sound of Liam's voice, pasting a smile on my face. He was standing in the middle of the office doorway with the light from behind surrounding him like a glowing halo.

Those flutters in my stomach I mentioned earlier began to gather into a flurry of excitement once again.

The good ol' sheriff's bod wasn't your Christmas gift this year, Miss Naughty. I brought you a fresh mouse, remember? Still alive, I might add. Do you know how that goes against my more basic instinct?

"Liam, I was hoping that you'd still be here."

"Sorry about that," Liam apologized, gesturing behind him with a wave of his hand. "I was finishing up a phone call. Let me guess. You need a coffee fix after all that tea, right?"

Did I ever.

I guess I should explain Liam's observation so you're not confused.

Yes, I own the tea shop that I'd inherited from my grandmother. There was a slight problem with that scenario, though, because I preferred coffee.

Okay, I loved coffee.

Let me rephrase...coffee was, in fact, the nectar of the gods.

You have a serious problem.

"I do need a coffee fix, but Heidi is waiting for me in the car. I don't want to keep her too long."

I took a few steps closer, realizing that I hadn't actually thought this through.

I swear, do you ever think things through?

How was I going to ask for the old case files on a fifty-three-year-old murder without coming across as a bit odd?

Do you really want me to comment on the insanity of that request?

"Is everything alright?" Liam asked with concern, taking a step forward so that his handsome features came into sharper view. I suppressed the need to fan myself. "Is your battery giving you trouble again? You really should have Newt take a look at the charging system for you. This cold weather can be potentially dangerous if you don't take the proper precautions."

I remained silent while I thought through my current plight.

Please change your mind, please change your mind, please change your...

I closed the distance between Liam and me while ignoring Leo's pleas. He was getting his whiskers tied in a knot over relatively nothing. What could it hurt to look into an old murder with the good intentions of clearing Nan's name?

What's the worst that can happen?

Now that *I can answer. Do you want the first possible cata-strophe or the hundredth? Forward or backward? You pick. I can even put them in alphabetical order, if you like.*

"My Corolla is just a bit temperamental," I replied with a casual shrug, ignoring Leo's bait to focus solely on Liam's suggestion of a mechanic. In all honesty, I was lucky my old girl was still running. And no, it had nothing to do with magic. "I was hoping to ask you for a favor of sorts."

"Anything you need," Liam said, returning my smile with one of his own. He shifted to the side with an invitation to enter his office, which I graciously accepted. I might have sucked in as much air as I could while walking past him. His cologne was like an aphrodisiac that caused me to pause mid-stride. "You know, I was a bit concerned that you might be going to cancel our plans. I am sorry that I had to postpone our date earlier. My sister, Meghan, was the only one in line the day spontaneity was being handed out. She got an abundance."

See? He's a fuddy-duddy. Even he admits it. Cancel and let's go.

I tried not to appear too distracted by Leo's continuous interruptions, but that wasn't always an easy thing to do. With that said, I was getting better at it. A quick glance around the office reassured me that he was still invisible, so at least I had that going for me.

"What's on your mind?" Liam asked, his voice akin to my favorite beverage in the morning.

"Well, I was talking with Cora Barnes about some of the reasons she and my mother don't quite get along." I didn't bother to take a seat in one of the two guest chairs, knowing Heidi was probably chomping at the bit already. It wouldn't surprise me if she left the Corolla running while she came looking for me. "Cora said—"

"Let me guess," Liam interrupted with a small frown. I was just getting to the good part, too. "Cora brought up the unsolved murder from fifty-three years ago."

Here we go...you know I don't look good in stripes.

"How did you..."

I let my voice trail off as I realized that nothing was sacred in this town. It was honestly a wonder how Nan had managed to keep her witchcraft under wraps for so long. I tried not to be disheartened that these townsfolk knew more about my family than I did.

I can relate. Memory loss is nothing to sneeze at, you know. It's a serious disorder.

"Yes, it is about that unsolved murder," I replied to Liam, confirming that he was spot on. He had no idea I'd used witchcraft once before to solve a murder, and there was no reason I couldn't do so again. A zing of anticipation shot through me at the chance of closing this case before bedtime tonight. "Cora mentioned that she and my mother had a falling out over Nan's alleged involvement."

I explained this earlier, but I was now able to sense things around me. The air tended to crackle with energy and my palm became warm when there was danger nearby. There were also times when a slight resonance could be heard to forewarn me when a conversation was about to veer in the wrong direction.

Yeah, that didn't happen this time around.

"My mother went to high school with Cora and your mom," Liam revealed, leaving me a bit speechless. How had I not known this before? "My mom and Regina were rather close before your mother left for the city. One might have even referred to them as best friends."

Is this where you humans drop the mic?

No, that wasn't a mic drop in the least.

Unfortunately, I couldn't explain that to Leo right at this moment. I was too shocked at the fact that Liam's mother and mine had been BFFs.

Another thing occurred to me.

Leo had to have known that little tidbit of information.

Short-term memory loss, remember? It's an affliction. I thought we already discussed this.

Another conversation to have at a later time—there was a big difference between short-term and long-term memory loss.

Oh, my Supernatural being! Did your grandmother not read the label before casting that black magic spell?

"You've never mentioned your mother before," I said softly, catching sight of the pain that flashed in Liam's dark eyes. The last thing I wanted to do was hurt him with my interest in the past. "I didn't mean to—"

"It's all right," Liam reassured me, shifting on his worn brown boots so that he was leaning back against his desk. "It's not a secret that my mother grew up in Paramour Bay. She passed when I was in middle school. Cancer. Meghan was a senior in high school, but she wasn't eighteen years old at the time. Otis and his wife took us in when social services would have put us in the foster care system."

All of this explained so much, especially why Otis was so proud of Liam. He'd followed in his guardian's footsteps as protector of Paramour Bay.

"Anyway, Mom and Regina had a falling out with Cora and Beverly Garber. There might have been a fifth girl involved at the time, but I don't recall her name offhand." Liam tapped a finger on the desk as he thought it over. "Meghan was having problems with a group of mean girls at school. Mom explained the story of how Cora had said some awful things to Regina about your grandmother's role in the murder of Norman Palmer. Of course, the lesson was that words can damage long-standing friendships. We can all learn from their example."

Norman Palmer.

Liam had brought up the name once before in connection with Nan. In turn, I'd asked my mom about the man. I'd gotten the feeling that Nan had been intimately involved with Mr. Palmer, and I even had my own suspicions about his identity. It didn't take witchcraft to figure out that fifty-three years ago was the time that Nan had been pregnant with my mom.

Let's just say that particular conversation with my mother hadn't gone over so well.

"Raven, what's this favor you wanted to ask of me?" Liam inquired almost cautiously, as if I was about to wish for the moon and stars.

"I wanted to read over the old case file," I admitted, deciding I might as well jump into the deep end with both feet. I held up my hand when I got the sense that Liam was trying to figure out a way to turn down my request. "Before you say no, what is the harm in letting me take a peek at the reports? Otis was the one to investigate Norman Palmer's death, so I know that all of the old paper files are still in this office."

"Raven, the murder took place fifty-three years ago." Liam rubbed his jaw as he most likely tried to come up with a way to turn down my request. "Your grandmother was a person of interest in the case, because she was involved with the victim. They had a relationship."

I knew it!

I refrained from pumping my fist into the air in an act of victory.

Truthfully, the only thing I knew about the investigation was that Norman Palmer was found floating face-down in the lake. I assumed he'd drowned, but I'd never asked about the cause of death.

"Otis called in the state police, but there were no other leads. The case was a dead end." Liam still hadn't said he wasn't going to give me the files, but I could easily sense that he was leaning toward denying my request. "Raven, Norman Palmer wasn't really a local. He'd been a guest at the inn for a little less than two weeks before his death. He told Gertie that he was just passing through, and his behavior didn't suggest otherwise. All the townsfolk who the state investigators spoke to agreed that he was just a nice guy who got caught up in something bad. He began courting Rosemary, and then one day he turned up dead."

There you go. All the information you need. Now let's go before you muddle this up.

A few things stood out in the facts that Liam had just related to me, but the most vivid one was that Norman Palmer couldn't have been my grandfather if he'd been in town for only two weeks. Nan had been pregnant at the time of his visit.

He wasn't my grandfather.

"No wonder Nan was a person of interest," I murmured, more to myself than Liam. Had Nan had something to do with Norman Palmer's murder? What if I delved into this old case only to find out that my grandmother was a murderer? No. No, I didn't believe that for a second. "Liam, please let me look over the files. I promise to give them back at the beginning of the week."

Are you purposefully doing this to ruin my New Year?

"Raven..."

Liam let his voice trail off, almost as if I exasperated him. I didn't understand his reluctance to open the files to me, but maybe it had to do with Otis' involvement. Had he or the state police missed something within the investigation? Otis had been friends with my grandmother. Had he covered up a crime of passion to save my Nan?

Why is it that you always allow your imagination to run away with you? Can't you take the good ol' sheriff at his word?

The case led to a dead end. So, we should leave well enough alone before you set fire to the past.

This entire time I'd been under the assumption that Norman Palmer was just an average male who'd succumbed to murder by another average everyday human being. Leo's vexation with my interest in this case now had me guessing that Nan wasn't so much the culprit as the cause.

I'm leaving now. I've got an itch behind my ear. And Heidi's been waiting too long in the car. You realize that doesn't make you a very good friend, now does it?

I was definitely onto something.

"Fine," Liam relented, shaking a finger at me. "You can have the weekend to look over the file, but then I'd like the reports back in the same condition I gave them to you. All of them. Every page and photograph."

"Deal."

There was no hiding my bright smile, and I adored the way he shook his head with minor amusement. The last thing I'd want is for him to think I'm boring. It was always better to keep men on their toes...or claws. For some reason, Leo came to mind. He might complain a lot, but he'd had more adventure in the past two months than he'd had in a lifetime with Nan. Well, maybe. The answers I was looking for all depended on what these old case files produced.

"I was curious about the murder myself a time or two," Liam said as he walked over to one of the filing cabinets in his office. He fished out his keys before easily choosing the one he needed. "It was the only crime not solved in Paramour Bay. Otis took it personally. It's the reason I keep the case file in my office instead of the archive storage room over at the county building."

"I find it hard to believe that every other crime to have

taken place in Paramour Bay has been solved." I wasn't questioning Liam's abilities as a sheriff, but it was highly doubtful that any law enforcement agency had that type of closing rate. "Aren't there some kind of awards for that?"

Liam's rich laughter filled the air, but the sound was much more soothing than any Christmas carol. I was beyond happy to be going with him to the New Year's Eve party.

"It's not like we have a large population, Raven. Not much gets past these townsfolk."

Liam's words instantly slammed into me and the palm of my hand began to tingle. I'd been looking at the black and white clock on the wall above Liam's credenza, wincing at the fact that Heidi had been waiting in the car for so long. I hadn't realized that he'd already collected the files.

He was watching me closely...too closely.

It was almost as if he believed I had the answers he was seeking.

Did he know that I was a—

"Raven Lattice Marigold!" Heidi suddenly appeared in the doorway with a frown on her pretty face. The flurries caught in her blonde curls began to slowly disappear one by one. "We're going to run out of gas if you take any longer in here, and my toes are about to fall off. The heater in the car suddenly stopped working ten minutes ago."

There wasn't a doubt in my mind that Leo was behind Heidi's interruption.

He'd done something to my Corolla so that Heidi would have no choice but to come in here in the nick of time.

I definitely didn't give him enough credit.

"Your car heater is out with these temperatures?" Liam asked, his worried gaze shifting from Heidi to me. "Why don't I drive you home? We can have Newt look at your vehicle first thing in the morning. I know he sometimes works on Saturdays, and this way he can look over the entire vehicle to make sure it's safe to drive in the first place."

"She's just temperamental," I reassured Liam, knowing full well that Leo would have the heater back up and running by the time Heidi and I walked outside. "I know exactly where to hit the dashboard to get the heat to come back on. I promise."

If Liam's arched brow was any indicator, he didn't believe a word that came out of my mouth. I couldn't blame him, but it was technically the truth.

That counted for something, right?

"You have my cell phone number," Liam reminded me, taking the two remaining steps between us. He handed over three thick files bound into one murder book, but he didn't immediately release them. He waited for me to make eye contact with him before issuing another directive. "Please call me if you break down before reaching your house. I wouldn't want to spend New Year's Eve alone."

I couldn't prevent the rosy flush that no doubt cascaded over my cheeks.

"I promise that I'll call you if we run into any trouble."

The files in my hand were heavy, but at least my palm was no longer tingling. I guess I had Leo to thank for what could possibly have been a very awkward conversation. There was no doubt that Liam suspected something was amiss, but did he believe that something was with me or with my dearly departed Nan?

"I'll pick you up at seven o'clock on Monday," Liam reminded me with a small wink. I relaxed somewhat as I nodded my acknowledgment. Putting things into perspective, what was the worst thing that could happen should Liam find out the truth? It wasn't like he could arrest me for being a witch. "You two drive safe and remember to call me if you run into any problems I can help you with."

"We will," I assured him, joining Heidi in the doorway. There was one more thing I needed to do before we could leave. "Liam?"

I turned around to find that he hadn't moved from where I'd left him. He was rubbing the small growth of whiskers on his chin, most likely still wondering what the missing pieces of the puzzle were in regard to the Marigolds.

"Thank you for letting me look at the old case file," I said softly, holding the manila folders close to my chest.

"You're welcome, Raven Lattice Marigold."

I thought maybe I'd been the one to audibly sigh at the way he'd said my full name, because goosebumps washed over my body as if I'd just stepped into a hot shower. It was clear that he'd been attempting to mimic Heidi in good jest, but his voice almost set fire to the murder book in my hands. Fortunately, the distinct sigh came from Heidi, saving me from embarrassment. As I fell into step with her, it didn't surprise me when she commented on the obvious.

"I call dibs on being your maid of honor. Leo will have to fend for himself."

Three

"I HAVEN'T EVEN GONE on a date with Liam yet, so don't you go making any plans that would have my mother being admitted to the hospital for a stress-related illness."

I parked my Corolla—amazingly with a working heater—parallel to the black wrought iron fence that surrounded the front half of my property, no longer fazed by the eerie sight of the old Victorian-style cottage.

You might think I'm being overly dramatic using the word *eerie* as an adjective, but I'm right on target considering its resemblance to a classic haunted house. I wondered why Nan fostered the idea of the foreboding exterior visage, yet she'd spared no expense at updating the interior.

It struck me so instantly upon opening the front door for the first time—the foyer and great room were spacious and inviting, and the kitchen was modern with granite countertops and stainless steel appliances. Nan and her penchant for under-stated appearances made me speculate about what she could be hiding other than the obvious. Peering out through the windshield brought all these thoughts to the forefront in light of what discoveries were to come.

The porch light I'd left on highlighted the overgrowth of entangled vines that were now nothing but thin, creepy twigs. The wrought iron fence with sharp spikes and the two bare trees on either side of the house didn't take away from the ominous appearance, either.

It was all an elaborate façade.

Or it could be that Nan just had a wicked sense of humor.

"Your mother did mention that she wasn't thrilled about who you had a date with for New Year's Eve." Heidi had been holding her hands in front of the heated vent, and she groaned in displeasure when I turned off the engine and her current source of pleasure. She quickly unfastened the seat belt and reached for the door handle. "I don't get it. Liam is handsome, sweet, and nothing like the guys you dated in the city. You'd think she'd be happy for you."

I should probably take offense to that narrative, but I guess I couldn't argue. My track record with men wasn't the best. In all honesty, it might have been the fact that I kept meeting them in bars rather than at the library.

My mother had always said the worst place to meet a man was in a bar.

"Mom doesn't like Liam based solely on the fact that he lives here in Paramour Bay. She doesn't want me here period." I pressed the button on my seatbelt and then opened my door. The cozy heat inside immediately escaped with a brief swirling gust of wind, forcing both Heidi and I to move quickly. "You know that she wants me back in the city where she can keep an eye on me. Mom doesn't want me to have anything to do with her hometown. She associates anything and everything in Paramour Bay with her rejection of witchcraft."

Heidi and I both opened the back doors of the Corolla at the same time. The freezing crosswind coming off the bay took my breath away, forcing me to snatch up the files I'd set in the backseat as Heidi grabbed her bag. I closed the door quickly and brought the thick stack of papers to my chest to help ward off the cold.

A quick glance at Leo's favorite window told me he wasn't inside just yet.

Where had he gone, and what was he doing this late on a Friday night?

He'd yet to make an appearance after he'd fiddled with the heater on my car. He probably wanted to avoid a lecture, but I wouldn't give him one this time since he'd fixed it before we'd gotten back in the car for our trip home. Plus, who knows where the conversation with Liam would have ended up if Heidi hadn't come into the police station when she did?

Leo had actually done us both a favor.

"Your mom certainly didn't take it so well that I'd been included in on the family secret." Heidi finally joined me with her purse and a small suitcase in hand. We fell into step side by side and started for the gate. "Now that I think about it, she hasn't returned the message I left her."

"Give her time," I suggested, knowing that my mother always came around in the end. "Mom also said that she'd never have anything to do with witchcraft again, but she was the one who helped Leo teach me how to correctly channel the energy I derive from my environment to create the magic I utilize in my spells."

I pulled the gate open just as Heidi let out a bloodcurdling scream.

My heart rate tripled, and I immediately released everything in my hands to take the defensive stance that Heidi and I had learned in a self-defense class we'd taken years ago. My palm immediately began to burn with its need to vanquish whatever we were about to face.

"Ted!" I admonished, not surprised when the endearing giant revealed a couple of broken teeth in his attempt to smile. "One of these days, I'm going to put a bell on your lapel."

"A bell?" Ted asked, taking me seriously. He looked down at his suit jacket in confusion. "I'm not sure it would ring properly against this fabric."

I leaned down to gather some of the papers that had slipped out of the manila folders. Liam had been smart to wrap a rubber band around each of the thick files to keep everything in the larger three-part binder. It was the only thing that had saved the majority of the case's documents from being saturated with the wet snow.

"Hi, Ted," Heidi greeted him as she patted him affectionately on the arm after catching her breath. "How are things going?"

You're probably wondering who or what Ted is, why I referred to him as a gentle giant, and why he takes everything I say so literally.

Bottom line?

Ted came with the house.

Seriously.

I inherited him with the house just like the rest of the oddities I've received since my arrival here in Paramour Bay.

I'm not kidding. At first, I'd thought Ted was some type of caretaker who lived in the outbuilding in the backyard. Turns out, he's a...

Well, I'm not exactly sure what Ted is.

He lives in a small shed located adjacent to the water that borders the back of the property. His verbal skills might be limited, but don't let him fool you. He's as sharp as a tack. He's highly intelligent, kind, somewhat naïve, and would do absolutely anything for me without question.

He was also close to seven feet tall—okay, more like six feet and six inches—and had yellowish blond hair and pale sunken eyes. Between you and me, there's a good chance he wasn't human. I kept putting off that discovery, because there was only so much of the supernatural that I could take on any given day.

"What did you do to Leo?" Ted had taken over holding the gate open. It was rather irritating, but the hinges didn't squeak when he opened and closed the entrance like it did for everyone else. "He's been inside meowing and pacing back and forth on the coffee table."

Ah, so that's why Leo wasn't lying on the windowsill.

"Leo got upset with Raven when she decided to look into an old murder case that happened some fifty-three years ago," Heidi shared, finally making her way up the sidewalk. I was right behind her, unable to feel my nose after having been outside for far too long. "Can you believe that Leo even fiddled with the heater in the car so that I would go into the police station after her? I'm thinking Leo knows more than he's letting on about what happened back then."

"Leo always knows more than he lets on, but his short-term memory side effect that came from the dark magic Nan used prevents me from finding out anything very useful." I'd kept the keys in my hand, so it didn't take me long to unlock the front door. "I still haven't had time to look through all the boxes up in the loft. There has to be more about my family history in some of those papers. Ted, do you think you could—"

Ted was gone.

He'd snuck off the moment he'd heard about my plan.

Why?

Because he's smarter than your average henchman.

"Leo, what is going on?" I asked, wondering if he'd remembered something from all those years ago. From my understanding, Ted had only been around for ten years. "And don't try to get out of this conversation, either."

"Ted certainly is quick for such a big guy," Heidi muttered, looking around the front yard for any sign of the giant. She then closed the front door with a shrug. "Okay. Break out the wine. I'll go change into my pajamas, and then we can veg on the couch looking through those files. Oh, and don't upset Leo. He's my little lover kitty."

I love her outlook on life.

I knew this to be a fact, and I didn't have the heart to break it to him that Heidi had her sights set on Detective Jack Swanson of the state police. He was escorting Heidi to the New Year's Eve party at the wax museum, which was liable to break Leo's heart if he was willing to subscribe to reality.

"Does Ted know something about the murder?"

Of course not. He didn't exist back then.

Exist?

Now that was an odd choice of words.

I bit my tongue to prevent myself from being baited into asking what Leo meant. He'd been waiting months to tell me what Ted was in this supernatural world I'd found myself caught up in, but I wasn't ready to hear it.

Instead, I carefully set the files on the entryway table and dropped the car keys in a ceramic bowl next to a matching vase. I'm pretty sure they cost more than what my vintage Corolla was worth.

Nan liked the finer things in life, and she absolutely adored expensive quality items. I'd discovered her jewelry box just the other day. I'd never sell even one piece of the sets of jewels I'd found hidden away inside, but I did tell my mother about the little collection of treasure. Those types of things should stay within the family, some of which should be my mother's.

As for the cottage, well, I hadn't changed one thing to the interior of Nan's home. My home, now that I agreed to stay here in Paramour Bay and take over the tea shop. I still had trouble reconciling that all of this was mine, because two months ago I'd been struggling to pay the rent in New York City.

To find myself owning a tea shop, a home that was beautiful on the inside, and being left to care for two odd supernatural characters was quite astonishing.

I'm not odd...exactly. I prefer unique.

That much was up for debate.

Anyway, the cottage was technically one level with a bedroom loft over the kitchen and a small root cellar. The modern appliances and furniture were interspersed with antique tables, pestles and mortars, and the most stunning hand-carved coffee table in existence.

Rosemary is to blame for my flawed personality. I was quite the premium familiar back in my day—a special friend to a powerful practitioner.

"I don't doubt it, Leo." I hung up my dress coat on the antique coat rack next to the entryway table and then began working on taking off my boots. Leo was still pacing back and forth on the coffee table, clearly irritated we were even having this conversation. "You're like the Encyclopedia Britannica for the supernatural world, although you're missing a table of contents. Any type of index, for that matter. You were also with Nan during the time of that murder, so you've some idea of what transpired back then. Your memories are just locked away, which got me to thinking that—"

Stop right there, missy. I still haven't gotten over the tail-numbing incident. I'd rather have my whiskers pulled out one by one before allowing you to use another haywire spell on me.

"But it wouldn't be black magic," I reassured him, trying to recall if there was something in Nan's spell book that could undo the damage done to Leo's memory. I wiggled my sock-covered toes once both boots were on the mat next to the front door. "I don't understand why Nan didn't try it on you after your...traumatic experience."

Rebirth? My ascension to a higher form? Just what are you trying to say, Raven?

I wasn't going to attempt to describe Leo's transformation quite like that, but his depictions would suffice for the moment.

You cannot undo the repercussions left behind by black magic. There are consequences for disturbing the fabric of life. Otherwise, they wouldn't be called repercussions, now would they?

"I'm not giving up on retrieving your memories," I declared before gathering up the files Liam had so graciously given me. "In the meantime, we can go through these crime incident reports to see if we can pick up anything that might clarify Nan's involvement."

She wasn't found guilty. Is that close enough? Rosemary wasn't even arrested. Do we really need to dig her up and slap the cuffs on? She's far past caring about what happened all those years ago. See? There. How simple was that? Your grandmother's name is clear, and we can move on so you can actually learn something useful.

"Leo, you and I both know the residents of Paramour Bay believe Nan had something to do with this man's murder. I mean, it was part of the reason Mom left town and rejected magic."

You're missing the point by a country mile.

"And what is that?"

I don't remember.

I couldn't help but smile when Leo's memory loss came into play once more.

"Wine time!" Heidi had come down the spiral staircase that led up to the loft where she'd gotten changed into a pair of pajamas that she'd had for as long as I could remember. The vibrant cyan color had faded into a light baby blue. "Are you two still arguing about Rosemary's involvement?"

"We're not arguing."

Debatable.

"I was explaining why I believe it's important that we solve this old case." I left the files beside Leo and walked over to the counter. I took a seat on one of the stools while Heidi retrieved two wine glasses. "Leo doesn't believe we should look into the files, which tells me that Norman Palmer's murder might have had something to do with witchcraft."

"Have you thought of the alternative? That there might be a chance that your grandmother actually was the one who killed Norman Palmer?"

Heidi gently set a bottle of red wine next to the crystal glasses, clearly waiting for my answer.

Have you?

Both Heidi and Leo were now baiting me to say aloud what I adamantly refused to believe of my grandmother—that she could be a cold-blooded murderer.

Four

⧳

"I CAN'T KEEP my eyes open," Heidi declared dramatically with a groan, flopping back on the couch in a theatrical pose designed to demonstrate her level of exhaustion. "What time is it?"

"Almost one o'clock in the morning. Well past witching hour." I rubbed my eyes, hoping to ease the stinging sensation that had begun over an hour ago. "I think you're right. We should just go to bed and get a fresh start in the morning."

After reading through the reports that Liam had so graciously allowed me to look over for the weekend, I'd attempted a spell to recall the few moments before Norman Palmer's death.

Unfortunately, the incantation hadn't worked and all I could picture was...well, I think it might have been water. Technically, it was a rippling darkness. It would certainly make sense given that Norman's cause of death had been officially ruled as a drowning by the county coroner.

For once—okay, maybe Leo had done it twice before—he

had praised my efforts, telling me that I'd done the spell perfectly.

That was the thing with magic. One couldn't always count on the results he or she would obtain. It was more of an art than a science.

Leo had explained that the surrounding environment at the time of Norman's death could have affected the vision I expected to see. Events like recent electrical storms or meteor showers could cloud the results, just as bright sunny days could amplify the duration of my sight.

So why couldn't I see past the darkness?

"I don't get it, though." Heidi gathered the file she'd had in her lap and tossed it to the floor before turning on her side. I'd chosen to sit in front of the fireplace for the additional warmth, though the remaining flames were barely swaying above the cindered block of Hawthorn. It was a good slow-burning wood that provided plenty of heat. "Your grandmother was six months pregnant with your mom when Norman Palmer was murdered, yet she went out on three dates with him during the two weeks that he was in town. Maybe your biological grandfather found out and it made him angry. It's a track we haven't considered. The question is if it made him mad enough to kill."

The townsfolk assumed *the meals Rosemary shared with Norman Palmer were dates.*

I swung my startled gaze up slightly to where Leo was stretched out on the top of the couch behind Heidi. His eyes were most of the way closed, though the left couldn't shut all the way due to its enlarged nature. He'd been quiet for the last hour, so I had assumed that he was still sleeping. He hadn't commented once while Heidi and I were combing through the crime reports.

"Do you remember something specific, Leo?" I asked

cautiously, not wanting to scare away any memories that he might be recalling in his sleepy haze. "Was Norman in town to see Nan because of her special herbal remedies?"

Heidi pulled a funny face as she slowly looked over her shoulder, also realizing that Leo's recollections could be quite precarious.

Norman came to town to see Rita Carter, not Rosemary.

"Who is Rita Carter?" I quickly picked up the yellow pad of paper that I'd written every name down in association with the murder investigation. A one Rita Carter was not listed. "Leo, she was never interviewed by Otis or the state police."

Would you look at that? Could I have just given you a break in the case?

Leo literally had a Cheshire grin gradually appear underneath his twisted whiskers.

I do remember a few things from that time long ago. Yes. Yes. It's all coming back to me now.

"What do you remember, Leo?" I shifted so that I was on my knees, eagerly awaiting the next words to drip from his crooked fangs. I then rested my elbows on the coffee table as I concentrated on Nan's familiar, who had a wealth of information stored in that tiny feeble brain of his. We just needed to figure out a way to get to it. I attempted to coax him a bit more. "Was Rita a local?"

Oh, yes. She was quite revered back then, you know.

Leo reached forward with both paws and sank his claws into the microfiber of the couch as he stretched his back and his awkwardly bent tail. It was clear that he was very pleased with himself, especially when he purposefully sat in a regal position.

Rita Carter was Alison Bend's mother. She used to own the town's wax museum.

"Why wasn't this listed in the reports? You can't tell me that Otis didn't know about the connection between Norman and Rita." I automatically reached for my glass of wine, but it was long since empty. Even though I was currently experiencing a shot of adrenaline, I wasn't about to open up another bottle this late in the evening. "Do you know why Norman came to town to see Rita?"

Fred.

"Fred?"

Fred.

"Who's Fred?" I asked, obviously needing to clarify the reason I'd repeated the name in the first place.

You know Fred?

"Leo, I don't know who Fred is," I exclaimed, unable to hide my exasperation. "That's why I'm asking you who he is."

I don't remember. What were we talking about?

I let my head fall to my arms in defeat. I stayed draped over the coffee table until Heidi broke the silence.

"I'm just throwing this out there, but is there a spell for me to be able to hear Leo?" Heidi asked, laying back down on the couch and rubbing her temples. "The two of you give me a headache listening to one side of your conversations."

"Maybe there's a Fred on the suspect list," I muttered, finally sinking back on my heels and reaching for my trusty yellow pad of paper. "Fred, Fred, Fred...nope. No Rita or Fred."

"I don't understand why my spell didn't work," I complained, knowing full well that I sounded like a petulant child. I blamed it on the fact that it was one o'clock in the morning. "What other incantations could I do to get a glimpse into the past, Leo?"

Leo moaned in pleasure, and this time it had nothing to do

with his memory. He'd curled up in Heidi's lap, who was scratching underneath his neck in long strokes. He was useless to me now.

"Tell me who Otis had on the suspect list."

"Well, I've got five names. These people weren't technically suspects, but they were considered persons of interest and interviewed in addition to Nan and Gertie. Can you believe that Gertie owned the inn even way back then?" My toes were beginning to fall asleep in my current position, so I settled back down onto the plush off-white carpet that complemented the living room furniture. "Let's see. The five are Monty Leete, Albert Wignall, Eugene Tuttle, Trixie Fredericks, and Pearl Saffron."

"Monty, as in the Monty you tried to knock off?"

I don't think I've ever seen that exact shade of purple before in all of my nine lives.

"I did not try to kill Monty," I defended myself while considering getting rid of the ginger and peanut oil-infused tea blend altogether. It certainly wasn't one of my best sellers. In fact, most folks have avoided it like the plague since Monty's adverse reaction. And before you ask, yes...that's why I'd put that flavor inside the gift bag. I thought it would be a big holiday seller, and it wasn't. I'm not proud of that reasoning, mind you. "You're forgetting about Pearl's hair, Leo. The purple shade on Monty's face was very similar to Pearl's hair dye, if you recall."

Hmmmmm.

Leo wasn't acknowledging me in the least. He was still thoroughly enjoying the affection that Heidi was bestowing on his rather abnormal body of ragged fur.

"Why were they considered persons of interest?" Heidi asked with her eyes closed. Leo was now draped over her chest with his head nestled into her shoulder. "And aren't Albert and Eugene the two older gentlemen who play chess in the front room of Monty's Hardware Store next to that potbellied stove?"

"Yes, that would be them." I scanned the reasons why each person was interviewed, but there was nothing substantial that would cause me to believe that any one of those people committed murder. "Monty was interviewed because Norman had come into the hardware store looking for a crowbar."

"What did he want with a crowbar?"

"Otis asked that very same question." I had jotted down some notes between each suspect who had been interviewed. I tilted the page slightly to read my handwriting, which tended to become illegible when I was tired. "Monty stated back then that he never questioned his patrons as to why they purchased the tools they did. Additionally, the crowbar was found in the back seat of Norman Palmer's vehicle after the murder."

"You said the two chess players were interviewed." Heidi shifted a bit on the couch to become more comfortable, but she never opened her eyes. "What did they have to say?"

"Both are retired now, but Albert used to be the groundskeeper of the B&B. He and Norman got into an argument after he accidentally backed over the wood tie in the lot and into one of Albert's rosebushes." I squinted to try and decipher what I'd written after Eugene's name. "Eugene worked at the pharmacy, and there was a heated exchange when Norman stopped in to try and process some film. The photographs had all come out too dark to make out what was in the pictures. Eugene blamed the exposure setting on the camera."

"Trixie was interviewed because Norman wasn't happy

with one of his meals and created a ruckus at the diner, while Pearl..."

I had to smile at the fact that the older woman with purple hair had worked as a teller in the bank. Pearl's attitude made sense now. I don't know about you, but I always feel like the tellers behind the counter are judging me when I make deposits or pull out money—judging me for my lack of saving money rather than spending more frugally.

"Pearl apparently put Norman in his place when he came waltzing in the bank with a two-thousand-dollar out-of-state check. It says here that he was trying to cash a check from another state, but that he didn't have the proper identification. Nor did he have a bank account at our bank to cover the check if it didn't clear." The identification thing was odd. If Norman Palmer had driven into town, why wasn't he at least carrying a driver's license? "Maybe Norman Palmer wasn't who he said he was in the first place."

I quickly found the report where Pearl had been interviewed.

"Ah, it turns out that Norman claimed to have lost his wallet the first week he was in town. Pearl still refused to cash the check, claiming it was against the bank's check-cashing policies. Norman didn't take the denial all too well." I winced at reading what happened next. "He took a bunch of deposit slips off the counter and threw them into the air like confetti. Why would Nan be having dinner with someone who acted like that?"

After my inquiry was greeted with silence, I changed my question.

"Why is no one joining me in this conversation?"

Upon receiving no answer, I found that Heidi and Leo were both fast asleep on the couch. Leo had fallen in between

Heidi and the cushions, all four paws wrapped around her forearm. He certainly wasn't the average housecat, but the drool coming out of the side of his mouth was a bit much.

Heidi was no better.

She was definitely a mouth breather, producing a tiny snore to match his rhythm.

I finally postponed my quest to figure out who murdered Norman Palmer, but only for tonight.

Tomorrow was a new day, filled with promise.

There had to be an incantation somewhere in Nan's spell book that would allow me to get a peek into the past.

Worst case?

I'd have to call my mother.

Five

"...CRAZY to have come up with that idea," Regina Lattice Marigold exclaimed over the phone.

I'd put my cell in the middle of the kitchen counter, ensuring that the call was on speaker. I didn't want to be a one-woman audience for one of my mother's infamous lectures.

Don't worry.

She'll calm down soon.

"Heidi, I realize that this all must be rather exciting for you, but rest assured that it is very dangerous dealing with powers you can't possibly understand. Being a witch is a curse, not a gift. It comes with a lot of responsibility that..."

"Don't you dare," I warned Leo with barely a whisper, putting my hand in front of him so that he couldn't use his paw to hit the cell phone. "We need her help."

You need help, alright. What were you thinking calling your mother for assistance when she despises the idea of you practicing witchcraft in the first place? I can do without her nonsense. Why do you think Rosemary left me here? It wasn't because of all the fresh air and open panoramic views.

"How long will your mother go on like this?" Heidi murmured as she poured both of us another cup of coffee. Unfortunately, no amount of caffeine was going to rid me of this killer headache from last night's bender while poring over the case file. "I was hoping to go into town today to find a dress for New Year's Eve."

"...can't believe that Cora brought up our feud to begin with," Regina all but bellowed, continuing her tirade. "That's between us, and she had no right to..."

"I thought you were bringing that black dress you bought on sale this past summer when the winter clothes were on sale?" I whispered back, taking the time to sip my freshly brewed coffee. I'm pretty sure my toes curled and my eyes rolled into the back of my head as the rich flavor slid down my throat. The caffeine did nothing for my headache, but the delicious beverage caused my mood to lift slightly. "Didn't it have ruffles on the sleeves? Also, the local business owners all decided to close up shop this weekend. Remember? Well, with the exception of Trixie's Diner and the gas station."

You're being quite rude to allow Regina to carry on like this.

"And it wouldn't have been rude to hang up on her? I swear, you're impossible."

It would have been much more efficient.

"Did Leo just tell you to hang up on me?" It was a good thing Regina didn't practice witchcraft anymore or Leo might have lost another whisker or two. All three of us leaned back from the counter, just in case. "You tell that mangy little—"

"Mom, I'm not defending Cora Barnes in the least, but she did apologize to me for her behavior toward you." I motioned for Heidi to bring me the yellow notepad I'd set near the coffee maker. "Cora technically isn't the reason I'm looking into

Norman Palmer's murder. I still notice some of the residents watching me with that suspicious look in their eyes, and I believe it has something to do with Nan's role in the unsolved murder case. I mean, she was six months pregnant with you when she was dating Norman."

Rosemary wasn't dating Norman Palmer. Good grief.

"Your grandmother did not *date* Norman Palmer," my mother replied irritably, clearly still worked up from the moment I'd initiated the call and explained my predicament. A glance at my screen revealed we'd been talking for twenty-four minutes and nine seconds. It certainly wasn't a record, but she had gone on nonstop for quite a while. "Your grandmother said she'd gone to dinner with Norman to discuss his interest in her herbal remedies."

See? I told you Rosemary and Norman weren't dating back then. Why do you never believe me?

"So, Nan *did* talk to you about Norman." I shared an excited glance with Heidi. I'd told her that Mom would eventually open up about her past. "What else did Nan say?"

"Raven, did you know that you were two weeks overdue?"

The question came out of nowhere. I began wrapping my hair around my finger to buy me some time to figure out how to get this conversation back on track.

"I did know that," I admitted reluctantly, having been told that particular fact multiple times in my life...usually when my mother was mad at me. "Mom, do you realize that Albert and Eugene look at me as if I have a third eye in the middle of my forehead every time I walk past the hardware store?"

Oh, that's only because they think your grandmother reincarnated herself.

I was going to argue with Leo about how insane that

sounded, but he might have a point with that one. We Marigold women all have long black hair, green eyes that are practically iridescent, high cheekbones, and rather full lips. Trust me, they aren't as glorious as those actresses in the old movies portrayed them to be.

"What do those old fools know, anyway?"

My mother hardly ever talked out of turn about another human being—unless that individual was Cora Barnes, of course. Anyway, I could tell that Mom was close to making a trip to Paramour Bay in order to try and drag me back to the city. Nothing was going to ruin my date with Liam, so I figured I'd best come up with a way to end this call while gaining as much information as I could glean.

"Raven, what I'm getting at is that you've always been stubborn and you're being even more obstinate now. Just hearing you mention Norman Palmer's name makes me break out in hives. Remember, I had to live with that same shadow of guilt my entire childhood. My mother moved to Paramour Bay when she was three months pregnant with me, which means she'd only been in town for three months before Norman Palmer showed up at the tea shop asking questions. I was born three months after his murder."

Why is it that I remember that clearly, but I can't recall what I had for breakfast this morning? Wait. Did *we eat breakfast?*

"I guess I never gave the timeframe much thought," I responded with a frown, ignoring Leo. Sometimes I forget that Nan moved to Paramour Bay because of a disagreement with her sister over my grandfather—who I still don't know anything about. Not even his name or if he had any involvement with the case. "You don't think Aunt Rowena had anything to do with Norman Palmer coming to town so soon after Nan moved here, do you?"

Please don't mention that woman. I remember her as clear as day, too. She dislikes cats. Who dislikes cats, I ask you?

Leo shuddered, causing a couple of stray orange hairs to hover in the air before floating down to the hardwood floor to mark his passing.

"My mother never spoke with Aunt Rowena after that, so it's highly doubtful Norman Palmer had anything to do with our extended family." My mother's huff of exasperation came over the phone quite clearly. "Raven Lattice, don't you go looking for trouble with those people."

"I'm not," I said defensively, relaxing a bit now that my mother's tone didn't contain so many daggers. Heidi went back to icing the cinnamon rolls she'd taken out of the oven after topping off our coffee cups once again. "You have to admit it's odd that Norman Palmer took Nan out on three separate occasions to talk about herbal remedies."

"I recall Mother mentioning that Norman Palmer was also interested in the history of the wax museum. He might simply have been a businessman looking to invest his money into Paramour Bay. Who knows? And I can assure you that your grandmother had nothing to do with his murder."

Could Norman's presence here in town have been that simple? Had he been looking for investments?

"Then why would someone kill him?" The dots weren't connecting, and I had a tendency to like all my ducks in a row. "It doesn't make sense. And who was Fred?"

"Fred?"

"Yes, Fred." I was getting a sense of déjà vu. "Leo mentioned a Fred last night before his slate went black. Was Fred a local?"

I remember Fred.

"Really?" I whispered harshly to Leo, wishing he'd said something sooner. What was with this Fred guy? "Would someone please tell me who Fred was?"

"We're getting a bad connection, dear."

Heidi snorted the coffee she'd just sipped all over the cinnamon rolls, though I didn't find my mother's attempt at dodging my question funny in the least. Plus, Heidi had just ruined my breakfast.

So, we didn't have breakfast is what you're telling me.

"Mom, don't you dare hang up on me. You heard my question as clear as day." I grabbed my cell phone and brought it closer to my mouth. "Who was Fred? There's not one person listed in these crime reports with that name. Mom? Don't you dare hang up that phone!"

"What was that? I can't hear you, Raven." I could literally hear my mother tapping her nail on the phone. Did she really think that would actually work on me? "I'm hanging up now. Call me tomorrow. Ta-ta."

By this time, Heidi was laughing uncontrollably while Leo casually cleaned those bent whiskers of his. I turned all my focus on him, considering he'd said his memory had returned.

"Leo." I was very careful to keep my tone even when all I really wanted to do was take him by the ears. "Who is Fred?"

Fred is dead.

"I figured Fred was dead, since no one living in town has that name. But he was obviously alive at some point around fifty-three years ago," I reminded him, resting the palms of my hands on the counter in order to make eye contact with Leo. "What was his connection to the wax museum? Was he related to Rita Carter?"

Heidi was laughing to the point of barely breathing while I

did everything I could to hang on to my patience. It wasn't wearing thin at all. It was about to snap.

Fred worked for Rita.

Victory!

"So, Norman came to town in order to talk to Rita about Fred...who, in turn, worked for Rita. Do I have those facts correct?"

Leo's whiskers twitched.

It was his telltale sign that he was losing what memories had returned.

What facts were we discussing?

This short-term memory loss was turning into full-on amnesia when it came to certain time periods in his life.

Catnip might help. I'm certain of it. Where's my pipe?

"You disappear for hours at a time when I give you catnip," I complained, wishing witchcraft wasn't so complicated. Why wasn't there a spell to reverse the consequences of black magic? "Maybe we should call Mom back and—"

Between Heidi and Leo both shaking their heads and cutting off my suggestion with a chorus of *nos* loud enough to break glass, I decided they might be right.

That left me with only one course of action.

"Heidi, let's finish getting ready and then head into town for a real breakfast."

"Wait," Heidi said a little breathlessly, still trying to control her laughter. She even wiped the corners of her eyes with a dishtowel. "I thought you said none of the shops were open."

"They aren't, but Alison Bend will be at the wax museum getting the place ready for the New Year's Eve party on Monday night. We can stop by after..." I arched a brow at the drenched cinnamon rolls as I walked past with my coffee cup in hand. "...we eat at the diner."

My last suggestion might have had an ulterior motive, because Otis usually had most of his meals at the diner. At least his memory was intact.

I heard that.

Besides, what could it hurt to ask Otis a few questions about this mysterious Fred?

Six

"I HAVE ABSOLUTELY no idea who you're talking about," Otis adamantly denied, wiping his salt and pepper mustache with a paper napkin. "There was no one with the first name of Fred connected to the murder investigation. And I should know. I was twenty-two at the time, and I remember that case as if it were yesterday. Now, I know what you're thinking—that's pretty young. What town would hire someone so inexperienced to be sheriff, but no one wanted the job. It so happened that I had just completed a degree in criminal justice. It only took me three and a half years, because I was driven to complete the program. I stepped up to the plate with more confidence than I should have, not knowing then that I would have a dead body on my hands in my first month on the job."

I winced when Otis' animated voice carried throughout the diner, alerting every patron to our conversation.

Sure enough, several heads turned in our direction.

The rumor mill was blowing out the cobwebs.

I couldn't force myself to look over my shoulder at Eugene and Albert. I'm fairly certain they were probably both glued to this not-so-private discussion.

Not to squirrel when Otis was finally revealing information about the case, but I'd really thought the man was in his late sixties when we'd talked before. I quickly did the math to come up with the ripe old age of seventy-five.

Holy cow!

I hope I look half as well preserved at the age that he does.

A thought occurred to me.

Had Nan been sprinkling some of Cora's aging blend into Otis' arthritis blend?

It made me wonder just how far Nan had gone with playing witch doctor to these good folks here in Paramour Bay.

"These are the best pancakes I've ever eaten," Heidi murmured around the oversized bite of food she'd just shoved in her mouth. Her eyes rolled in blissful pleasure. "Seriously, have you had these?"

I'd ordered the same breakfast plate, but I was too concerned with the conversation to really develop an appetite. Being the first one to get bundled up this morning after talking with Mom, I'd made a quick detour to the backyard to find and speak with Ted. He hadn't answered my knock on the shed door, and I couldn't make anything out through the drapes that hung over the frosty windows.

Where could he have gone this morning?

I know it's odd, but Ted usually visited Mindy's boutique shop to check out a mannequin she had on display. Mindy swore that the gentle giant was in love with the woman-sized doll, but her shop would be closed today.

Ted also didn't drive, and we were a fair walk from town... especially in this wickedly cold weather.

"Where did you come up with that name from, anyway?" Otis asked, his curiosity clearly piqued as he dragged my attention back to the conversation at hand. He pushed his plate slightly away from the edge of the table so that he could rest an arm on the laminate surface as he swirled the toothpick dispenser with his other hand in preparation for selecting the right one. "Norman Palmer was murdered fifty-three years ago. It's not like people still find the time to talk about that cold case."

I took Heidi's advice and shoved a forkful of pancakes in my mouth to buy myself some time. My saliva glands immediately sprang to life. What in the world did the chef put in the batter?

More importantly, what was I going to say to Otis?

Did I mention that I decided to use my newly discovered talent for witchcraft to solve our town's only unsolved murder case?

I did, didn't I?

Yeah, that hadn't gone over very well.

Nothing was apparently going to stand up to the task at hand, because no spell I found could show me the last few moments of Norman Palmer's life. The one I'd used hadn't been very effective, and Leo didn't know of another one that I could garner the information I wanted.

Wait a second.

What if Leo really *did* remember what happened all those years ago? What if he was pulling one over on me similar to my mother's dodge that she'd tried to pull on the phone this morning?

There could very well be an enchantment hidden in Nan's spell book to pop his cork!

"I've already explained that Cora came into the shop

yesterday and brought up what happened between her and my mother," I managed to say after swallowing the large bite I'd taken of the pancakes. Heidi was right. They were beyond amazing. A quick sip of tea and I was able to talk a little more clearly. "I know it sounds silly, but I think some of the townsfolk still believe Nan had something to do with Norman Palmer's murder."

On a side note, I *was* drinking tea. No one else besides Liam knew of my addiction to coffee. I had to keep up public appearances. Owning a tea shop came with responsibilities, and one of those was drinking the beverage I sold to the diner.

Trust me, I was still figuring out a way to incorporate various coffee blends into the shop's inventory. The name *Tea, Leaves, & Eves* made it rather difficult to add beans.

"I found no leads or evidence of any sort that implicated your grandmother was involved," Otis exclaimed, his bushy left eyebrow rising higher than his right. "And neither did the veteran state detective I called in on the case back then. He helped me in more ways than you can imagine over my first few years on the job. He's long since retired now and living somewhere in Florida, last I checked. I bet he's got himself one of those fancy boats for saltwater fishing."

It was a known fact around town that the only thing Otis might love more than his wife was fishing the local lakes. It was clear to see that he was going a bit stir-crazy this time of year, but he still wore his fishing hat decorated with flies and small lures.

We were really getting off-topic now—pancakes and fishing hats.

"Otis, I thought I saw somewhere in the reports that a man who went by the name of Fred worked for Rita Carter at the museum." Heidi nudged me, but I ignored her rebuke that I'd stretched the truth. Even my mother had gone to great lengths to avoid talking about this Fred guy. What was everyone hiding? "I found it odd that he wasn't interviewed or had a statement taken."

"This is what I recall, Raven," Otis declared, leaning forward to impart his recollection of the past. "Norman Palmer came into town unannounced. He stopped in at the B&B for a room at the seasonal weekly rate. He told Gertie that he wasn't sure when he'd be checking out. The man ended up staying in Paramour Bay for two weeks, during which time he spoke to Rita about the museum, your grandmother about her special herbal remedies, and ate three meals a day here at this very diner —even though Gertie served meals at the inn as part of his room and board. That man acted as if he was looking for something very specific, but he took all his secrets to the grave the day he died in the surf."

"Why was Rita never officially interviewed during the murder investigation, and what did Mr. Palmer want to ask her about the museum?"

I had a lot more questions, but those two were currently at the top of my list. Something was definitely hinky about the investigation, but it wasn't polite to accuse Otis of any improprieties. Come to think of it, Nan might have very well had a hand in the direction that Otis' questioning took. Hmmm. It was something to ponder.

"Rita was only in town for the first few days of Norman's stay at the inn. If I recall correctly, I added a line or two in there somewhere in those crime reports that she had left on her annual vacation to England," Otis shared, a fond smile growing underneath his mustache. "Rita used to bring back the best shortbread I've ever tasted from those trips. Shame that she finally passed on a few years back."

Heidi had nudged my side with her elbow three more times during my conversation with Otis, so I finally tore my gaze from his to see what was so important that it couldn't wait until we were alone. Her blue eyes were rather wide with worry and darting in the direction of the window.

Oh, my.

Ted was standing on the sidewalk, facing Mindy's boutique while holding a bouquet of flowers frozen stiff in his hand. He'd brought the mannequin flowers? My heart broke for him, and I couldn't allow him to remain outside in this cold weather pinning away for an inanimate object. I already had an odd enough reputation in this town without Ted adding his kooky behavior to the mix.

"I forgot my...my phone in the car," Heidi exclaimed, feigning a brief search of her purse. "Would you two excuse me? I'll be right back."

I debated allowing Heidi to be the one to go outside and retrieve Ted, but she'd already had a pretty decent cover story worked up. We couldn't both leave our breakfast plates half-eaten on the table, so I scooted out of the booth and allowed Heidi to do the same.

"Don't eat the rest of my pancakes," Heidi said jokingly, casually taking her dress coat off the silver pole that each booth had installed between them. "I'm coming back for those."

"She's got spunk," Otis praised, refocusing his gaze back on me as I reclaimed my seat. "Did you hear that old man Beetle is retiring? We're going to need a new CPA in town. Isn't Heidi one of those number crunchers kind of folks in the Big Apple?"

This was the first I was hearing about...wait a minute.

"Beetle? You mean the older gentleman who drives the red Volkswagen Bug?"

I'd seen the white-haired man driving into town every day, but I didn't know they referred to him by that nickname. Technically, I didn't know his real name, either. He obviously wasn't much of a tea drinker, but I did find the nickname rather endearing. Another thing I found appealing—really appealing—was Otis' suggestion about Heidi moving to Paramour Bay.

Now wouldn't that be something?

Having my best friend live so far away was difficult, but would she consider such a drastic change in her lifestyle?

My best friend was citified through and through, much like me, and I wasn't so sure she'd ever consider such a drastic move. The thing of it was, she spent at least two weekends a month taking the train from the city to come visit me. Could I convince her that it would be in her best interest for her to live in Paramour Bay rather than in New York City?

There were a lot of benefits to living in a small town, most of which were intangible. I could write down the advantages in order to prove to her that the pros outweighed the cons.

"Back to the old murder investigation, I don't believe there's much I can tell you that I didn't jot down in those reports. I was new to the job, and I recorded down everything I could think of at the time." Otis drank the rest of his coffee. "I'm sorry I couldn't be of much help."

"I appreciate you inviting me and Heidi to join you for breakfast," I said, meaning every word. Residents in Paramour Bay always took time out for one another, and that was definitely something I could include in the pro column for Heidi. I tried my best not to look out the window, not wanting to call attention to her efforts to corral Ted. "Being the newcomer in town can be rather difficult."

Otis appeared to want to say something, but he instead leaned forward so that he could reach for his wallet. He pulled it out of his back pocket, flipped it open, and pulled out a twenty-dollar bill and some ones.

He was paying for our meals.

How sweet was that?

Another added bonus I could tack onto the pros of Heidi's list to living in a small town was that the prices were beyond reasonable for three people to eat at the diner. A complete meal for one at the diner only cost five dollars and fifty cents. In the city, pancakes and sausage with orange juice would have been twenty-two dollars alone...and that was without the six-dollar coffee.

"Breakfast is on me," Otis said with a brief smile. His salt and pepper mustache which he'd decided to grow in the last two months made him look even more distinguished if that were even possible. He must have been quite the looker back in the day. One side of that mustache curled downward as he spoke. "Raven, your grandmother was a single pregnant woman who'd just moved to a new town around the same time Norman Palmer showed his face. It was a shame that she got caught up in that murder investigation, but the past is the past."

"Is it?" I quietly laid my fork on my plate, sneaking a glance at Heidi's cup of coffee. Would Otis know if I picked up the wrong cup? "Albert and Eugene still look at me suspiciously every time I walk past them over at the hardware store. My mother lost high school friends over those old rumors, and I know it still bothers her to know people believe Nan had something to do with Mr. Palmer's death. I'm sure it's part of the reason she left for the city."

I did want to clarify something before Otis left the diner.

"Nan told my mother that she and Mr. Palmer only ever talked business over those meals they'd shared before his death. Why did people believe they were dating?"

I steeled myself for any detail that would cause me to have a different opinion about my grandmother. It *was* possible that Otis had left something out of the reports he'd drawn up back then. After all, fifty-three years was a very, very long time ago.

I certainly didn't expect Otis to have an actual answer that left me doubting my mother's earlier account of Nan's explanation.

"Everyone saw Norman Palmer kissing your grandmother goodnight on the sidewalk after their last dinner together. It was common knowledge." Otis reached over and patted my hand, most likely to make sure I hadn't gone into shock. "As I said, Raven. The past is best left buried where it belongs."

Had I not seen Otis' lips moving when he gave me his advice about the past, I would have sworn those words came from between Leo's bent whiskers.

The past was best left buried.

It wasn't, though.

I had a renewed sense of purpose to clear my grandmother's name.

"Thank you for breakfast, Otis." I squeezed his fingers to let him know how grateful I was he'd answered all of my questions. "Will I see you Monday night at the New Year's celebration?"

"The missus and I wouldn't miss it for the world. It's our one chance to get all dressed up." Otis concentrated on folding his wallet and tucking it into the back pocket of his khaki pants. Before too long, he was putting his fishing hat back on and giving me a charming wink. "I hear we'll be seeing you there on Liam's arm, as well."

"Don't forget me," Heidi chimed in, saving me from saying something sappy to the man who'd done an amazing job raising a fine young boy into the man he was today. "I'm always up for a good party, Mr. Finley."

"Otis, dear. Call me Otis." He scooted out of the booth and held out an arm, kindly gesturing for Heidi to take his seat. "Raven and I were just discussing the benefits a small town could offer a person looking to relocate. I'm sure she'll fill you in on the details."

Otis and I shared a secret smile before he made his way to the exit, stopping at almost every table to tell other patrons he'd see them Monday evening or something similar.

Wouldn't it be fantastic if Heidi lived in Paramour Bay?

"Where's Ted?" I whispered now that everyone's attention was on Otis' departure. "I can't believe Ted walked to town in this weather. And where did he find those flowers?"

I suppose it was a silly question to ask, considering Ted was the one who somehow found every single ingredient I needed for all my various spells. He must have access to a greenhouse somewhere.

Seriously, where did one find fresh white rose petals in the dead of winter here in Connecticut?

"Ted is sitting in the car with the heater on, so we need to finish eating as quickly as possible." Heidi hastily slid her plate over while pushing Otis' toward the window. The ponytail she'd compiled high on her head swung back and forth as she scooted forward so we could maintain privacy. "And you know Ted. He didn't say much, other than he wanted to stop into the boutique. Do you really think he's in love with a mannequin? That's more than a little odd."

"No, I don't think Ted's in love with a mannequin," I admitted, my appetite finally returning. "I think Ted has a crush on Mindy, but he doesn't want her to know he's interested."

"You're probably right," Heidi admitted, giving Otis one last wave before he walked out the door. "So, what did I miss?"

"Nothing new, other than Otis revealing that Norman Palmer was seen kissing my grandmother goodnight, and that's the reason the town believes they were seeing one another."

A kiss *was* a kiss.

Maybe Nan *had* been falling for Norman Palmer.

"You do realize that everyone you want to speak to about the case is going to be at the party on Monday night, right?" Heidi wiggled her eyebrows as she took another bite of her pancakes. "We can divide and conquer. I bet when I tell Jack that we've been going over the old case files, he'll want in on the side action, too. Nothing like clearing a cold case to get you noticed."

I gave Heidi's suggestion some thought, coming to the conclusion that she might be onto something. Detective Jack Swanson would have access to the state police files compiled during Norman Palmer's murder investigation.

"That's not a bad idea at all, Heidi." I lifted my now cold cup of tea, more than anything wishing it were piping hot coffee. She clinked her mug to my cup in success. "Let's finish our meal, and then get Ted home before he becomes a mannequin all on his own. I was so afraid that he'd gotten lost that I—"

Yes! That's it!

A spell that could locate a lost item.

Yes, yes, yes!

"That's what we need," I exclaimed, making circling motions with my hand to communicate my need to hurry. "Heidi, Norman Palmer lost his wallet sometime during the two weeks he was here in town. I can cast a locating spell to find his billfold. Maybe wherever the wallet is found can give us an idea of who he really was and why he was even in Paramour Bay in the first place. This could be it, Heidi. This could be the break we've been searching for."

Seven

EVENING HAD FALLEN along with another inch of snow, and I was still without any solid answers.

There might be a reason for that.

As you can tell, Leo's catnip hangover had worn off from this morning. He was a bit crispy, as it were.

"Leo, you're not being fair. You know something about Fred that you're not telling me. Why keep it from me when you know I'll figure out his identity eventually?"

Sure enough, Leo's whiskers twitched at the mere mention of Fred's name.

"Did you know that your Aunt Rowena sent your grandmother a birthday card every year?" Heidi's voice floated down from the bedroom loft where she was currently sorting through one of the many boxes Nan had left behind with our family history. "There's a small sentiment written in each one."

"Do the messages include anything of importance?" I asked from my position in front of the fire place. I was once again seated between the hearth and the coffee table. I'd set out the pestles and mortars needed for the locater incantation, and I was currently flipping the pages of Nan's grimoire looking for various enchantments and charms that would help Leo's short-term memory loss—not that it was a problem at the moment. I'd come to the conclusion he wanted to keep certain things hidden from me for what he considered my own protection. "And is there a return address on the envelopes? Maybe I should reach out to her."

Crash!

I jumped to my feet, abandoning my relaxed position as my fight or flight instinct kicked in.

"Leo!"

Oops.

The ceramic bowl I used to hold my car keys was no longer. The mixture of beautiful swirls made up of burgundies and greys were now in shattered pieces all over the hardwood floor.

"Are you okay?" I asked, curbing my suspicion that Leo had knocked the bowl to the floor on purpose. "Don't move. The last thing we need is for you to slice open your paw."

I'll stay right here.

Here was the windowsill where Leo could monitor the outdoor activity. He'd been staring outside at the colorful string of Christmas lights Ted had strung around the wrought iron fence. We were quite a ways from town, but I'd still wanted a festive appearance even if the outside of the house made it seem like we were stringing decorations for a funeral.

"What happened?" Heidi called out, suddenly appearing over the wooden banister.

"Leo bumped into one of my favorite ceramic bowls," I replied, crossing the distance to the kitchen. There was a small closet off to the left where I kept a dustpan and a foxtail. "I've got it."

"Still no Ted?"

"Still no Ted."

Heidi and I had driven Ted home after breakfast, though he'd been very quiet. And I mean more than his usual three-word sentences. I was getting a tad bit worried about him, but he seemed to perk right back up when I mentioned I'd be needing ingredients for my spell.

Neither one of us had seen him since.

"Your grandmother didn't save the envelopes." Heidi was still leaning over the banister when I came back into view. "You can always try to look up your Aunt Rowena online."

Another crash resounded through the cottage.

"Leo!"

Both Heidi and I had called out Leo's name in unison. My voice contained a lot more frustration than it should have.

That one might *have been my fault.*

"I get it, Leo. You don't want me contacting Aunt Rowena. Stop breaking things," I grumbled, tiptoeing through the shards of glass. "You could have just said you didn't think it was a good idea. These were really nice pieces."

"And expensive!" Heidi called out, no longer visible as I began to sweep up the jagged slivers of glass. She must have gone back to the box of family papers. "Don't forget that small detail."

Would you have listened to me either way? "You'll never know now, will you?" I admonished, almost falling over when a loud knock came from the front door. "Darn it."

"Did you cut yourself? I swear you'd break a leg going down a single step."

"Yes," I yelled back at Heidi, holding my cut finger up so that I didn't get blood everywhere. "Don't you dare say another word."

Who...me? I'm the very incarnation of restraint.

"No, not you," I said, attempting to stand without hurting myself further. "Heidi."

"I heard that, you know!" There was a slight pause from my best friend before she asked the same question she usually did in this situation. "Do you need to go to the ER?"

Oh, Mother Nature, yes! It's my heart. I can't believe Heidi isn't spending New Year's Eve with me. It's got to be my legs, right? I mean, they're repulsive! They're much too stubby for my build. I'm disproportionate.

"No, just a Band-Aid," I answered Heidi, who thankfully couldn't hear Leo. "Leo, Heidi loves you just as you are, and that includes your stubby legs. No human could make her go all gooey inside the way you do when you purr and slobber all over her."

Leo's green eyes narrowed as he contemplated my opinion, which I thought was rather intuitive and kind given that I was bleeding in the middle of the living room due to his lack of finesse.

I had a tendency to be accident-prone myself, but more so in the city where there were more people to observe. Maybe it was because there were more people around to bump into, thus usually resulting in a coffee stain on every outfit hanging in my closet. My dry cleaning bill had almost been higher than my rent on a few occasions.

You know, you're right. Jack Swanson doesn't hold a candle to my enchanting charisma.

I might have just created a monster.

No, I take that back. This was all Nan's fault, beyond a shadow of a doubt.

Another knock came at the door.

"Come in!"

I wasn't overly surprised to see Ted, considering he'd disappeared nearly ten hours ago in search of my material components.

"Was that the vase?" Ted asked, taking in the scene before him. A wicker basket hung over his arm, similar to the way a waiter carried a folded napkin in a posh restaurant. I could barely contain my excitement at the thought of completing the locater spell. "I can clean that up for you."

"It wasn't me this time," I protested, giving Leo a sideways look in accusation. "It was Leo's way of telling me not to reach out to Aunt Rowena."

How was I to know that you'd listen to me without an exclamation point for once?

"Miss Rowena is not a very nice person."

Ted's declaration caught me by surprise. I recalled Leo saying that Ted had only been around for ten years. If Nan hadn't spoken to Aunt Rowena in fifty-three years, outside of an occasional birthday card, how would Ted know anything about her unpleasant demeanor?

"Hey, did you know that your great-grandmother's name was Rowena?" Heidi had taken her mission to search through the boxes seriously. "Your aunt must have been named after her."

There are only so many female R names, you know. It was bound to happen sooner or later.

At the rate Heidi was going, she was guaranteed to be an expert in the Marigold family lineage by the end of the year. And to let you know what Leo was referring to, every Marigold female's name begins with an R. I couldn't tell you where it started, though I'm sure Heidi was working her way toward a reasonable explanation at some point.

"Ted, how do you know Aunt Rowena?" I asked after managing to step over the remaining small pieces of glass. The end of my index finger was beginning to burn. "I thought she and Nan hadn't spoken to one another in decades."

"I answered Miss Rosemary's phone once."

That was Ted's first mistake.

I'd made it around the kitchen cabinet, fishing out the box of bandages from underneath the sink. Ted didn't continue talking, and it wasn't long after that I realized that's all he had to say on the subject.

"So, Aunt Rowena tried to call Nan?" I prodded as I ran my finger underneath the faucet of running water. "What did she say?"

"Miss Rowena or Miss Rosemary?" Ted asked, wanting clarification. He was using the small brush to expertly sweep the remaining glass into the dustpan without incident. I curbed my jealousy at his pain-free example. "Miss Rosemary's response was not what most polite people would consider appropriate."

Nan might not have been from New York, but no one could say that she hadn't spoken her mind.

"What about good old Aunt Rowena?" I dried my finger and chose a small bandage. "What did she say when she was on the phone?"

"Miss Rowena simply demanded to speak to Miss Rosemary."

Once again, Ted stopped talking as he finished sweeping up the glass. He straightened his tall frame and began walking very carefully toward my spot in the kitchen. I pressed the Band-Aid tight against my finger to stop my exasperation from showing.

Try spending ten years with him as your partner in crime.

"And you said?"

"I informed her that Miss Rosemary wasn't available to speak with her."

Ted opened one of the bottom cabinets and let the glass slide down from the dustpan into the garbage can.

By this time, Leo had slowly sauntered on his short legs into the kitchen. He wasn't quite that graceful as he leaped onto one of the stools and then onto the kitchen counter, nearly missing it entirely.

I remember that phone call.

"You do?" I didn't want to act too shocked at that notion, so I cautiously closed the lid on the first aid kit and put it back where I'd found it. "Anything interesting?"

Not in the least.

"Ted, what was Aunt Rowena's response?"

"She left a message about bread," Ted replied as he walked over to the closet and hung the dustpan and broom back onto the small hook. "Do you need anything else this evening, Miss Raven?"

"Bread? Really?" I often found myself repeating words over and over, but neither Ted nor Leo ever seemed inclined to clarify their answers. "Why in the world would Aunt Rowena call Nan after years of not speaking to one another over something like bread?"

"I don't know the answer to that question," Ted responded with a slight bow. "Good night, Miss Raven."

Leo and I both watched Ted as he took very deliberate steps toward the front door.

"Don't say anything nasty," I warned Leo before resting my elbows on the counter. "Ted tries his best. Do you know if Nan ever tried returning a call to Aunt Rowena?"

Do you mean by phone or something else, like sticking a needle in a voodoo doll?

"Voodoo?" I straightened quickly as Leo's words sunk in. "As in New Orleans voodoo? Are you—"

Leo made a torturous hacking sound that I'd only heard once before, mistakenly believing that he was about to throw up a hairball. He was laughing at my naiveté, and I quickly came to the realization that he'd pulled one over on me.

You're so gullible. It's like catching fish in a barrel...a very small barrel.

Eight

"YOU'RE MAKING ME NERVOUS."

Can a cat have asthma? I mean, I think I have it. Geez, if only Rosemary had succeeded in casting her spell properly, I'd be a Persian leopard right now. I wouldn't be having these ailments if I were a great big Persian leopard.

I was currently sitting on my favorite oversized pillow in front of the coffee table where all the ingredients Ted had brought me had been separated into several small grey bowls made of hand-quarried and shaped granite. These containers were older than the coven my grandmother escaped so long ago and contained a magic all their own...at least, according to Leo.

The matching pestle and mortar positioned in front of Nan's open spell book remained empty for the time being. Everything was set in order to cast the locater spell for Norman Palmer's wallet.

Maybe it's a panic attack. Yeah, that's what it is. I've had one or two of those before, you know.

Unfortunately, I couldn't concentrate with Heidi staring at me as if I were some lab rat in a maze, watching my every movement. In her defense, she'd only known about the Marigold lineage for a couple of weeks. This whole witchcraft thing *does* take some getting used to.

"I'm not doing anything to distract you, am I?" Heidi questioned from her spot on the couch. She'd covered herself with a blanket, propped her elbows on her knees, and rested her chin in both hands as if she were waiting for the feature presentation to begin. "And I gave you my word that I wouldn't try to record you doing a spell. See? My phone is all the way over on the kitchen counter."

Leo made a very strange sound that came from the back of his throat.

For a brief second, I wondered if he'd misdiagnosed his asthma slash panic attack for something more serious—like a kitty heart attack. A quick glance revealed that his left eye was bulging more than usual, meaning that Heidi's request to catch me on a video casting a spell was definitely causing him some stress.

"Close your eyes, Heidi," I demanded, needing a bit of privacy for what I was about to do. "And keep them closed until I tell you to open them."

"Fine," Heidi muttered, settling back in the couch cushion and bringing the covers up over her shoulders. "You two are worse than my Grandma Ruth."

I'd met Heidi's Grandma Ruth, and Leo and I had just been insulted.

Don't get me wrong. I understand the evolving technological world and its immediate importance. We're surrounded by twenty-four-seven availability of anything or anyone. I'd done my homework on witchcraft. While there were many different sites out there to uncover and investigate, ninety-nine-point-nine percent of them were completely bogus.

The other point one percent?

Yep, you guessed it—witches who'd been ousted by their covens for going public.

"Leo, do I have a—"

Don't ask about things you don't want to know.

"But if there's a—

The Marigolds have always tended to work better on their own.

There was a story there, of that I was certain. Whenever Leo didn't want to talk about something, he always cut me off or pulled the memory gaffe.

I also don't want you to cast this spell and dig around in a world that is best left buried, but you don't see me complaining about my lot in life, now do you?

"Technically, you're—"

"Oh, would the two of you stop bickering back and forth?" Heidi was now in a bad mood, but that had everything to do with Leo and me taking away her fun for the evening. "How sure are we that this spell is going to produce what we want?"

"I'm not sure of anything," I replied with a frown, briefly considering that the reason the first spell didn't work was because of Norman Palmer's death being linked to the possibility of witchcraft. Now, after talking to Otis, I wasn't so sure about any of this. "Okay. Let's get this done."

I double-checked that the grimoire was still open to the locater spell before closing my eyes and breathing deeply, attempting to utilize the meditation skills I'd learned from my mother's brief tutelage. Who would have known how invaluable those few words had turned out to be? It made me wonder what I'd be capable of had my mother or Nan taken the time to teach me properly.

Anyway, the incantations took a lot of concentration and energy.

Would you stop explaining this ritual to the reader? They'll get to witness it firsthand if you just demonstrate it. Stop narrating everything.

I took another deep breath, and then another.

There were times when the initial energy needed for me to cast an enchantment just couldn't be summoned. Fortunately, I began to sense tingling in the tips of my fingers as the beckoning of my spirit drew kindred fuel from the environment around me.

I could only picture the aura as my own vision narrowed with the casting. The material components were all present, though the verbal and somatic elements were yet to be performed. But first, my focus was required.

Take the energy from the earth. Breathe it in, Raven.

Leo had technically been left behind to do exactly this—be my guide into the supernatural world. I might give him grief about the inconvenience of his memory loss, which was the cost paid for by the dark magic, but he was very good at leading me forward.

Let it travel up your arms, into your shoulders, and become one with your own energy. Accept the warmth of nature's power into your...

Leo's voice gradually faded into oblivion as my craft began to take hold. Only then did I open my eyes and focus on the scrolled text on the weathered page in front of me.

Not far from sight or mind,
do not be left behind.

I called out the first two lines of the spell, allowing my instincts to guide my hand to the rosemary Ted had brought along with various other herbs for binding, the delicacy of a flower petal's power, and the strength of the roots needed to complete the incantation.

With each stanza on the page, there was an ingredient written in Nan's handwriting. She'd discovered a method of her own to combine each component, and one that was very easy for me to adapt to as I carried on our lineage.

Once I'd read through the spell and all the ingredients were added to the pestle, I began to use the mortar to slowly macerate the ingredients with specific gestures in tempo. I continued to recite the enchantment until finally everything before me began to disappear leaving nothing but...blackness.

I'd come this far, though.

I wasn't going to stop when I knew without a doubt that the incantation was working and allowed me to get a glimpse of the past.

...channel the energy...

...focus on the item in question and...

...it will be revealed...

Leo's instructions intermittently broke through the veil, giving me the support my Nan couldn't be here to provide.

I opened myself up even further, drawing on the energy that was radiating throughout my body as it was provided from a bottomless pool. With as much conviction as I could muster, I chanted the entirety of the spell once again.

The blackness abruptly came into focus. But it hadn't been darkness I'd been seeing, but instead black leather. I held onto the power a while longer to get as many details as I could until the magic I'd created slowly seeped away, revealing a disbelieving Heidi riding on the edge of the couch with her mouth hanging open.

"That. Was. Incredible."

No, it wasn't. Tell her.

"But it *was* incredible," I corrected Leo, elation replacing the currents of energy slowly leaving my body. I sat back on my pillow, grateful for the warmth of the fire behind me. The disappearance of radiating power always left me chilled to the bone. "Even better, I know exactly where Norman Palmer's wallet is right this moment."

Well, you might want to explain to Heidi where good ol' Norman's wallet is currently at, because you're about to put all of us on another collision course with darkness.

Nine

"TOO PINK OR TOO RED?" Heidi asked, turning away from the mirror and pursing her lips for my opinion.

Too much. Tell Heidi not *to wear so much lipstick, and she should skip the gloss.*

"Too pink." I rummaged through one of my makeup bags, searching for the shade of reddish-brown lipstick I'd bought in New York City before moving to Paramour Bay. With my black hair, I usually stuck to my usual brown hues with just a hint of red. Too much red made me look like one of those mannequins that Mindy swore Ted was in love with at her boutique. "Try this. It's called Cinnamon Flair."

Lipstick gets on my fur, and I can't get it off. And gloss? Don't even get me started!

"Don't you think it's a bit odd that Jack is going to a New Year's Eve party here in Paramour Bay when he lives all the way over in New Haven?" Heidi asked before carefully applying the first coat of Cinnamon Flair to her lips after wiping off the too-pink shade she'd tried first. She rubbed her lips together and then leaned back to get the full view of her appearance. "I like this color, Raven. I might need to steal your supply."

What does Heidi see in Jack, anyway? He has no pedigree.

Jack was really a nice guy, but Leo wouldn't want to hear that right now.

No, I don't want to hear that tripe. Will he be man enough to bring her a live mouse?

"You can have that tube," I offered, ignoring Leo's comment about the mouse. He's never hurt one since I've moved in here and was really rather gentle with them when they crossed his path. Ted managed to capture the tiny grey furry creatures and remove them from my cottage without harm. "I have a similar shade."

We both put the finishing touches on our makeup. Leo had given a huff and left the bathroom, no doubt to go sulk by the living room window. I wouldn't allow him to start the New Year off feeling down, so I'd written down a spell that only required rosemary and a touch of catnip. Both the small piece of paper and the herbs were in my green purse to be used at the appropriate time.

"You've been awfully quiet since Saturday night," Heidi pointed out, leaning her right hip against the bathroom sink. "Raven, we have a plan in place to search for Norman Palmer's wallet. It will work. I don't see how it can fail."

Heidi wasn't wrong about a few things. One, I *had* been rather down since Saturday night. The locater spell had left me with a lot more questions than I'd had originally, which was saying a lot. Two, the incantation had left me with certain doubts regarding Nan's innocence. Three, which was totally unrelated to my latest quest, I was nervous about this evening's date with Liam.

I closed the bathroom door, not that the measly wooden

barrier could keep the pesky familiar out should he want to pop in. He could hear every thought in my head, but only if he was tuned in to me at the time.

"I'm beginning to suspect Leo is right about my date with Liam." There. I'd said my fear aloud. Unfortunately, my verbalizing the cause of my apprehension didn't lessen my anxiety. I moved past her to sit on top of the toilet. This certainly wasn't the most ideal place to have this conversation. "I'm a witch, Heidi. These past three months have been a whirlwind, and I think I've clung to the thought of a date with Liam to keep me anchored in the real world."

"So, what if you're an odd duck?" Heidi opened the shower curtain on its oval track so that she could sit on the edge of the claw foot tub. We were both wearing the dresses we'd chosen over the Christmas break, though she'd picked more of a cocktail-style dress than I had. Mine was longer with more flowing material, allowing me to wear my favorite knee-high boots with two-inch heels. At the end of the evening, it probably wouldn't matter what I had on. I'd end up in my pajamas with a quart of chocolate chip mint ice cream. "Raven, you've done nothing but grow as a person since you've been here in this town."

Heidi's observation had me raising an eyebrow, because we normally didn't have the *why are we even here* existential conversations.

"What do you mean?"

"I mean, three months ago you were passing strangers by on the sidewalk in the Big Apple without a thought as to who they were or what they were going through." Heidi had a wistful look on her face, which was currently framed with blonde curls. She reached out and took a hold of my hands. "Pearl walked into the shop yesterday, clearly upset that Henry still wanted to go to his winter home in Florida. You spent five minutes trying to figure out what the real problem was with her, only to discover she had a fear of getting on a plane. You promised to make her a tea blend that would ease her fears."

"And I can't share any of that with Liam," I explained, understanding just how much witchcraft had become a part of me. "Being a witch is a big part of who I am, Heidi."

"And you're just beginning to learn about the gift you've been given." Heidi squeezed my hand as she attempted to explain my so-called growth. It wasn't like I was a different person. "Don't you see? You never would have taken five seconds of your busy morning to ask the person behind you in line for coffee why he or she was upset. You—"

"Because they would have thought I was flipping crazy," I protested, not having been gone from the city that long. "People mind their own business in the city."

"Exactly. And now you're in Paramour Bay helping Otis with his arthritis, creating tea blends to help Wilma get over her cold, and helping Henry Wiegand realize that he loves Pearl with all his heart." Heidi gestured toward the bathroom door. "Leo and Ted are now an integral part of your family. You've created a life here, Raven. You are exactly where you belong."

I hadn't thought of my life in those terms, but Heidi was right. Leo just wasn't Nan's familiar anymore. He'd become my confidant and...my friend. I couldn't imagine my life without his incessant commentary and his quirkiness nor Ted and his peculiar slow and steady manner.

"But they accept me for who I am," I said, unable to stop the sadness from tainting my words. "Liam can never know about my lineage."

"Are you sure about that?" Heidi tilted her head, causing her curls to bounce. "The world hasn't ended with my realization. I haven't gone up in flames, and this coven Leo speaks about hasn't broken down your door to carry you away on a rail. Raven, you're going on a date. You're not getting married tonight, no matter how much I want to be your maid of honor. You're not sharing your deepest, darkest secrets. This new chapter in your life is just beginning, so allow yourself to have some fun—dinner, wine, a little dancing...and maybe, just maybe, a shared kiss at midnight, if you're lucky."

Heidi was right, which never ceased to amaze me. She usually came across as the spontaneous, carefree friend who would be the one using her one phone call from behind bars to say the excitement was all worth the price of admission. She would still do that, but there were times when she was able to help me see the forest before the trees.

"Thanks, Heidi." I leaned forward and gave her a hug of appreciation just as the doorbell chimed. I'd wanted to bring up Otis' suggestion about her taking over for Beetle this evening, but I'd run out of time. "You're the best."

"But do I look my best?" Heidi asked, both of us standing and giving our reflections a once-over for final approval. "Are you sure I shouldn't have done an updo? These curls are a little wild for a first date."

"Your blonde hair against the black fabric of your dress is what completes the package." I swung open the bathroom door and hurried across the hardwood floor. The bonus of living in a cottage like this was that it was a large open floor plan, not to say that there weren't a few hidden spaces. Within half a second, I was at the door. Would the man on my front doorstep be Liam or Jack? Both were picking us up separately. "Ready?"

No, not in the least.

Leo was in his usual spot in the front window with his back

to us. I hadn't told him of my surprise, and I wouldn't until the time was right.

"Ready," Heidi called out, the black ruffled sleeves of her dress making it look as if she were part of a coven that I wasn't sure even existed. "Wait."

Don't be preposterous. Of course, the coven exists.

"Are we sticking to the plan?"

Say no.

The plan had us searching for Norman Palmer's wallet in the wax museum, just as the locater spell had shown. The black leathered billfold wasn't in plain sight, but I did have a vision as to where it had been left. I assume Norman had been talking to Rita at the museum before she'd left for England, and he'd somehow dropped his wallet while engaged there. It was the only reasonable explanation as to why the billfold hadn't been found to date.

Just say no.

"Yes, we're sticking to the plan," I declared, unsure if mixing witchcraft business with pleasure was such a good idea. After all, I'd just gotten done telling Heidi that Liam couldn't know about my true identity. Alas, it wasn't like I'd have any other opportunity to search the museum the way I would be able to this evening. "Just don't get caught."

You are purposefully ignoring me.

I swung open the door so that I didn't have to have this redundant conversation with Leo again. He'd made his thoughts known, but in five minutes he'd forget all about this conversation.

You don't give me enough credit.

"Ted?" I'd been expecting Liam or Jack, but an unsmiling Ted stood on my doorstep. The unsmiling part wasn't unusual, but I could definitely sense his unease. "Is everything okay?"

"You must not go to the museum tonight."

Why doesn't Ted want you to go to the museum?

Sure enough, right on cue, Leo's short-term memory loss had kicked in.

"Not you, too." I slumped my shoulders slightly, because I really didn't want to get into an argument with both Leo and Ted on the night we were ringing in the New Year. I also didn't want to have a conversation with the door open. We were letting all the warm air out of the cottage and into the night, so I gestured for Ted to come in so I could shut the cold out and talk. Unfortunately, he remained standing on the doorstep, frozen in place. "Alison and Oliver Bend are hosting the town's New Year's Eve party. It would look odd for me *not* to be there. Ted, I realize the cold doesn't affect you as much, but I'm freezing. Come in out of the cold."

Wait. It's coming back to me.

"There was a reason for your grandmother's annual donation to the museum every year."

Ohhhhh, that reason.

Leo quickly stood on all four paws, his whiskers twitching uncontrollably.

You can't go to the museum tonight. I just remembered.

I tried to wait patiently for either Leo or Ted to continue, but I should have known that Ted's usual one-sentence thing wouldn't change just because we were standing in the doorway freezing solid. Neither would the fact that Leo was still trying to protect me from...I don't know what, because he wasn't being completely honest with me.

Shivers were now beginning to set in, and I was tempted to close the door in Ted's face.

You wouldn't dare.

No, I wouldn't.

"Ted, please come inside so that we can discuss this without me turning into an icicle," I practically pleaded before catching sight of a pair of headlights. "I insist. Hurry. Tell me why I shouldn't go to the party before Liam or Jack get out of their vehicles."

Jack is coming to the house? To pick up Heidi? How could you let this happen to me?

"Miss Raven, your grandmother did not kill Norman Palmer."

I could have told you that. Geez, this is really becoming silly.

Relief and frustration spread through me, though neither was enough to chase away the goosebumps that covered my body from head to toe. We'd been standing in the doorway for far too long, but Ted just refused to come inside.

"Raven, it's Liam," Heidi whispered after crossing the floor to come and stand beside me. She'd crossed her arms to keep whatever body heat she could, considering it now felt like the next Ice Age had begun inside my home. "You better make a decision quick."

It was beyond infuriating that these two had information that would give me peace of mind, but they both refused to give me the details so that I could make up my own mind.

Why?

Well, it's like on those television shows where the individual wasn't part of the crime, but they have to do the time, anyway. You see, being an accomplice can...

"Leo, I don't have time for one of your shaggy dog tales," I whispered, having heard a car door shut. "One of you tell me something useful before I leave for the party. And make it quick."

"Raven, is everything okay?" Liam asked, his voice carrying down the walkway. The gate made that horrible high-pitched squeak as he opened it to gain entry to the sidewalk. I was glad to see that I wasn't the only one who caused the hinges to make such a horrendous noise. "Ted, are you joining us this evening?"

"No, thank you."

The closer Liam got to us standing in the doorway, the more perplexed his expression became. I couldn't blame him. Ted was, as usual, not as forthcoming as he could have been, given that he was still staring at me with...sorrow?

"Oh, my," Heidi whispered, giving me a slight nudge with her shoulder.

I understood perfectly what she was referring to, because Liam looked dashing in his black suit with a tie that contained numerous beautiful green hues. His brown hair was combed to perfection, without a strand out of place, and his freshly shaven jaw made me want to place my hand on his cheek to see if his skin was as soft as it looked in the cold night. For just a second, I'd forgotten the reason Ted was standing on my doorstep.

I don't know how you could forget someone like Ted.

"Raven, you look absolutely stunning this evening," Liam complimented me, his dark gaze warming me just a tad. At least, until Liam's uncertain gaze landed back on Ted. "Is there something wrong, Ted?"

Yes. Very wrong, and it's all your fault for taking...

"I don't believe the party will be very fun," Ted declared over Leo's meows.

A second vehicle could be seen pulling off the main road and onto the gravel path that led to my cottage. Detective Jack Swanson had arrived to pick up Heidi, and I wasn't so sure he would be as patient with Ted the way Liam was on any given day. Heidi had summed it up perfectly a bit earlier—small towns were like a family tree, with many far-flung branches.

Raven, maybe we should get a hellhound. You know, one that I can boss around. One command from me and he would sink his sharp canine teeth into Jack Swanson's—

"Ted, Liam is taking me to the New Year's Eve party," I explained to the gentle giant as gently as I could while gesturing for Heidi to grab my dress coat. She did one better and also handed me the purse I'd chosen to carry, all loaded up with more than just rosemary and catnip. I'd packed an extra special emergency kit, just in case. "I hope you have a good evening here at the cottage. Please make sure Leo stays out of trouble."

On instinct, I raised up on my tiptoes and pressed a kiss to Ted's cheek. Of course, he had to lean down to receive it, but surprisingly enough he did. One of those rare, crooked smiles of his crossed his face.

"Goodnight, Ted. Goodnight, Leo."

Yeah, yeah. See you next year and all that jazz.

Liam shifted until he was able to pass Ted and take ahold of my dress coat. He held it open for me, allowing me to seek its warmth. It wasn't long until we were passing Jack on the sidewalk, who appeared only to have eyes for Heidi as he muttered a greeting in passing.

"Is Ted still standing at the door?"

I was afraid to turn around myself. Guilt had flooded my system, but I needed answers. If Leo and Ted weren't inclined to do that, then I needed to take matters into my own hands.

"Yes, he is," Liam replied after a quick glance over his shoulder while carefully guiding me around his personal vehicle that he'd left running to keep the interior warm. He usually drove the sheriff's SUV, but he'd traded it in tonight for a black F-150. Living in Connecticut, it wasn't feasible to drive anything without four-wheel drive...unlike my beat-up old Corolla. Maybe I could afford one of those Subaru sedans.

They had all-wheel drive. "Would you like me to walk back and convince Ted to join us? It feels wrong leaving him here like that standing out in the cold."

"You'd do that, wouldn't you?" I asked in bewilderment, adjusting my scarf so that the cold wind wasn't so harsh on my neck. We'd made it to the passenger side of his truck where he'd opened the door. "Ted is...different. Not a lot of people are comfortable around him."

"Ted's unique, but he's always offering his help to the townsfolk where and when needed," Liam explained with a half-smile, shifting so that his body protected me from the gust of wind. "Say the word, Raven. I'll go back and try to talk him into going with us."

I gave it some serious thought while I used the running board for leverage to get up into the passenger seat. It was beyond cozy and comfortable, making me wish we could stay inside the cab of his truck for the entire night, listening to the local radio station. I was able to see the front door through the driver's side window, catching sight of Ted standing there watching Jack and Heidi make their way down the sidewalk.

I wasn't too sure bringing Ted with us was the smartest thing to do. It was best to leave well enough alone, especially considering all the effort Heidi and I would need to put into locating Norman Palmer's wallet.

"Thank you, Liam, but I think it's best if we go to the party by ourselves."

And maybe, just maybe, there was something inside the wallet that would help me solve Norman Palmer's murder.

Ten

THE DRIVE to the wax museum had taken less than ten minutes on the slippery snow-packed roads, but Liam and I remained in the truck in the parking lot for a good twenty minutes discussing the very special yet eccentric folks who made up the small town of Paramour Bay. His recount of the town's history was interesting, but honestly, I could listen to him talk about his filing system at the station and still be fascinated.

There was something so genuine about him compared to the men I dated in the city. I guess he would best be described as *downhome*. Liam had an appeal about him that I found very attractive—he was comfortable. It probably sounds foolish, but he made me feel as if I belonged in this town with him and all the rest of the townsfolk.

"I never saw myself coming back to Paramour Bay, but not a lot of people were in line to take over for Otis," Liam revealed with a small shrug. I recognized that being responsible for the safety of Paramour Bay meant a lot to him. "Word around town has it that you signed a three-year lease.

What was it that changed your mind about selling the tea shop?"

"It's crazy, isn't it? Nan must have known by putting that caveat in her will about me staying a year before getting any proceeds from the sale of the tea shop would get me to change my mind about returning to the city." I couldn't share with Liam the entire truth of my reasoning, but I wouldn't lie, either. "My staying has nothing to do with the money. Had that been the case, I would have only signed the lease for one year. Paramour Bay, well, it's unlike any other place I've ever lived in before. I love the community, I love that one can be different here without criticism, and I really like owning my own business and working for myself. I think I must be more like my grandmother than my mother, but please don't ever tell her that."

"Your secret is safe with me," Liam promised, holding up the ubiquitous Boy Scout sign.

I was pretty sure by that devilish grin Liam bestowed on me that he'd never been a Boy Scout, but that didn't matter in the least. I could stay in this truck the rest of the night getting to know him.

Unfortunately, the parking lot was beginning to fill with folks passing by us on either side. It was a sure bet that the partygoers didn't appreciate walking through the exhaust fumes currently escaping his muffler, not to mention the gossip we would certainly be stirring up.

"We should probably head on into the party," Liam echoed my thoughts, though he didn't turn off the engine. The warm air flowing from the vents was like a cozy blanket being taken out of the dryer. I wasn't ready to go inside, not when we still had so much to discover. Maybe having our first date out with the entire town hadn't been the best of ideas. "Hey, did you have a chance to look over those files? I hope they were able to give you some type of closure."

"I wouldn't call it closure, but I did find out that Nan never dated Norman Palmer," I confessed after giving it some thought. It wasn't like that bit of information could get me into trouble or lead Liam to the truth about my lineage. Double-checking every word that came out of my mouth wasn't as easy as it sounded. "I happened to be talking to Mom on Saturday morning and brought up that I was interested in the case. I hate that some of the townsfolk believe Nan might have had something to do with that man's killing."

"Rosemary wasn't dating Norman?" Liam asked in confusion, having already disclosed that he'd read through the reports numerous times. He rubbed his chin in thought. "I was under the impression that they had quite a few meals together during his two-week stay, as well as—"

"The two of them being seen exchanging a goodnight kiss," I finished for him, recalling my conversation with Otis. "Nan told Mom that Norman was interested in the tea shop. The crime reports and Otis' notes do state that Mr. Palmer was also interested in the museum."

"Rita Carter passed away a few years ago." Liam tapped his thumb on the steering wheel. "It's highly doubtful that she said something about Norman Palmer to Alison, but I guess you could ask her sometime this evening. It's a shame his killer wasn't captured."

I'd made a mental list of questions I wanted to ask numerous people who were supposed to be in attendance tonight, but this really wasn't the time or place to bring up unpleasant memories. We were supposed to be ringing in the New Year, and out with the old. In this case, many years old.

Maybe I could wait to inquire about the investigation and

just focus on locating Norman Palmer's wallet. The killer had gotten away with murder for so long, what was another day or two?

It did occur to me that I hadn't once thought about the billfold since Liam had picked me up at the house. There was something so calming about his presence that I tended to believe everything was right in the world when he was around.

It wasn't...technically.

I wanted to clear Nan's name, but I also really wanted to be able to tell Liam the truth about my family's history. I was surprised to find my fingertips tingling, followed by a sudden warmth that developed in the palm of my hand.

"Oh!" I couldn't prevent the exclamation from spilling out of my mouth when a rather loud knock came at my window. A hand over my chest did nothing for my racing heart. Liam recovered more quickly than me and lowered the passenger window from his side to reveal the former sheriff. "Otis, you almost scared me to death!"

"No one's going to die tonight," Otis replied with a smile, his nose a bit red from the bitter cold. "This evening is all about celebrating with good friends and ringing in the New Year with a smile on your face."

"That it is," Liam replied with a regretful grin my way as he reached for the keys in the ignition. Oddly, the warmth of my palm began to fade. "I guess that's our cue to head on inside."

Otis didn't hesitate to open my door and offer his hand, leaving me no choice but to follow his lead. I'd wanted to suggest to Liam that we schedule a second date on the calendar where we could talk the night away, but it was looking as if I'd missed yet another opportunity tonight.

"I left my better half inside. She was worried when we pulled in behind you twenty minutes ago and the two of you didn't follow us inside." Otis made sure I was safely out of the truck before closing the door behind me. "I didn't mean to interrupt anything coming to a boil."

"Liam was filling me in on the founders of Paramour Bay," I shared as Liam appeared beside me, holding out his arm for me to take. Alison or Oliver must have had a service come and ensure that the parking lot to the museum was clear of any ice, because the black asphalt was glistening in spots underneath the streetlights where the sand or salt had melted the snow. "The history of the town is just fascinating."

"My parents were born and raised here, taught me the values of right and wrong, and I'm proud to have served a community that is as close-knit as we are." Otis leaned past me to open the glass door of the museum, which I have to admit I've never had the time to visit. The one-story building was rather large, but I guess it would have to be to store wax figures from years past. "You know, Rita used to throw these get-togethers to ring in the New Year many years ago. Tonight sure does bring back a lot of old memories."

Was it bad of me to think Otis meant that declaration somewhat differently than the context of the conversation? He had been twenty-two years of age when Norman Palmer was murdered. Had the newly elected sheriff at the time of the crime gone above and beyond his duties to keep his citizens safe from harm?

I didn't want to think that someone I knew could be an unrepentant cold-blooded killer.

Liam opened the second glass door for me to step over the threshold, revealing—

Welcome to the 1920s and every decade that followed.

Nothing like making a grand entrance.

Leo's appearance—more like vocal appearance—had me

tripping over the metal plate that separated the small entryway from the main area of the museum. Thankfully, Liam caught my arm and helped me regain my footing before my entire body could be sprawled out on the cold, white tile lining the foyer in front of me.

"Raven, are you okay?" Liam asked with concern, handing over door duty to Otis. "That was a close one."

Another couple came out of nowhere, right on our heels. Liam and I moved to the side to let them pass, thus giving me more time to gather my composure.

What was that rascal of a familiar doing here at the New Year's gala?

You have to ask me that? I was enjoying a pipe full of catnip when I suddenly remembered that you're going to try and find Norman Palmer's wallet tonight. I have no idea how I could have forgotten such a dire expedition into the wild, but I've come to stop you from making a huge mistake.

Liam's concerned gaze was still on me, but I figured it had more to do with my look of horror that Leo was somewhere in this building than it was with my health.

Of course, I'm in the building. Where else would I be at a time like this?

"Did I mention that I was a bit accident-prone?" I made my question into more of a quip, hoping Liam didn't notice that my laughter wasn't exactly genuine. How could it be? I was a horrible actress, which made my life rather difficult when Leo suddenly appeared out of nowhere. That didn't stop me from glancing down at my boot and feigning displeasure, although I was equally bad at lying. "Is there a restroom close by that I could try and get these salt stains out of the leather with some hot water?"

Leather? Good lord.

Leo was right, but would Liam notice that my boots weren't made of real leather?

He's the sheriff, dear. And here I thought I was the one with short-term memory loss.

"Yes, the restroom is across the hallway on the right. If you find yourself in a singer's lounge of old crooners, you've gone too far," Otis replied, pointing to a sign overhead in the far corner. He patted my shoulder before scanning the crowd. "Liam, I'm off to find Karen to let her know that the two of you are alive and breathing."

My gaze had followed Otis', and the view left me breathless. Wow.

Being here was like being transported back to another time.

I was sure that when the museum was conducting business, wax figures of famous men and women were strategically positioned throughout the main area. In their place were two mini-bars stocked with chilled champagne and various hors d'oeuvres and a main bar on the other side of the room. There were a large number of round ten-seat tables surrounding a dancefloor with a slightly raised wooden floor. Even colorful party hats and favors had been sprinkled around the tables to give the otherwise historic interior a splash of color.

Even with those major changes to the décor, nothing could alter the nostalgic atmosphere this place emanated from years past.

The venue was perfect for a New Year's Eve gala.

I'm not so sure. That Frank Sinatra wax figure doesn't come close to doing the man justice. You know, he was a close personal friend of mine in a past life.

A familiar scent greeted me, and it wasn't Leo's story.

I guess I'd been too busy trying not to fall flat on my face, but now that I was able to get my bearings, the inside of the museum smelled of...lemon-scented Pledge?

My mother used the polish on our wooden furniture when I was little, but I couldn't figure out why a wax museum would have such an unusual odor.

You mean your mother didn't twitch her nose and have the dust magically disappear? How inconvenient for a domestic goddess like your mother.

The twitching of the nose was a standing joke between Leo and me regarding witchcraft in reference to the old television show, but I didn't find it humorous at the moment. He was supposed to be at home, safe and sound. He certainly wasn't supposed to be at this party where his short-term memory loss could be triggered at any moment, allowing himself to materialize in front of all these guests walking among the hors d'oeuvre trays.

What excuse would I use then to explain his presence?

I, unlike someone else we both know, have complete control over my supernatural abilities.

"Are you sure that you're okay?" Liam still had a hold of my elbow. A part of me wished I didn't have to leave his side, but a conversation with Leo was definitely in order. I recalled not three weeks ago when Leo lost his so-called control over his ability to appear or disappear. "No broken toes or rattled nerves?"

We were almost killed! There are exceptions to every rule, you know.

"You're not getting out of dancing that easy," I promised Liam with a smile, in awe of my newfound ability to manage two conversations.

I was definitely getting better at multitasking.

Not really, but we can argue about that later after you kick

Dudley Do-Right loose. Right now, you need to drop your interest in Norman Palmer's murder.

I pointed up to the ceiling to draw Liam's gaze from mine. A very large silver disco ball was currently hanging from what were hopefully well-secured fasteners of some type. The way my luck was going, that thing would fall on my head before midnight. We'd have our own dropping of the ball.

Don't tempt me.

"Good to know that you're still up for a little partying," Liam replied, his dark gaze settling on me once more. He was reading me better than my acting skills could defend. I needed that restroom break.

Maybe I could request a special song for us.

Might I suggest "I Shot the Sheriff"?

"May I take your coats?" a sweet voice asked from behind what normally would be a counter where one would pay for his or her tour of the museum. And just in time, too. I was ready to start lashing out with my newly salt-covered boot in hopes that it connected with Leo's backside. "Raven!"

"Kimmie, it's so nice to see you again!"

The young woman was none other than Alison and Oliver Bend's granddaughter, and she'd inadvertently saved Leo from my well-deserved wrath. I was beginning to think that Nan had intentionally gotten the spell wrong to keep Leo on this plane of existence.

I expected Leo to chime in, but there was only a contemplative silence.

"It's good to see you, too." Kimmie tore a ticket off a large roll, handing it over to Liam. "I love your dress. And those boots are to die for. Sorry about the sodium chloride all over the parking lot. We wanted to avoid the lawsuits and ambulances tonight."

Rosemary would never have done something so mean.

My exchange with Kimmie had given Leo some time to reflect on what I had thought, which had been the whole point.

Unfortunately, Leo had recovered a little too quickly for my comfort level.

Shame on you for suggesting such an underhanded devious plan. Your grandmother may not have been a saint, but she was a talented witch in her own right. She wasn't as fortunate to be born under the same grandiose sign you happened to be graced with, but she'd earned every accolade the coven had bestowed on her prior to her abrupt departure.

"You look fabulous, too. I love your sense of style," I complimented Kimmie, meaning every word. Her blonde hair was up in a stylish bun, and her dangling ruby earrings matched the vivid color of her dress. Her bright smile told me that things were going better than the last time we'd run into one another. "How have you been?"

"Couldn't be better. Grandma Alison is paying for a friend and me to go to New York City next weekend," Kimmie exclaimed with excitement as she took Liam's coat. I set my purse on the counter, allowing Liam to help me out of my dress coat. I was happy that I'd chosen to wear long bell sleeves with a long flowy skirt given the chill in the air. I'd mentioned it before, but these types of museums tended to be a bit on the cooler side due to the wax figures. "I have a huge list of art galleries and museums I want to visit. I'm fairly certain we won't be able to see them all."

"Come by the shop to see me before you go, and I'll give you a list of restaurants you can't miss while you're there. I've got the inside track wired on all of them." It didn't escape my notice that both of us thought the grass was greener on the other side. I truly hoped that Kimmie found what she was searching for in the Big Apple. I'd been there and done that, and I was very content with my new life here in Connecticut. Nor did I miss Leo's reference to my birth sign and the significance he'd failed to mention before now. I swear, it was like diving for pearls. You only found the special ones by chance. "Your grandparents have outdone themselves with this party tonight."

"Kimmie, don't forget to check out The Back Room," Liam suggested, joining in on the conversation. He was talking about a rather historic landmark in New York City. I'd totally forgotten about the fact that he was a graduate of the NYPD police academy. There was so much I wanted to ask him about his past, but I was once again realizing that maybe this type of gathering hadn't been the best venue for our first date. "I know you love history, Kimmie. Trust me, you'll be blown away by the speakeasy theme. The Back Room was where all the gangsters liked to hang out back in the heyday of prohibition, from Bugsy to Lucky. I'm pretty sure your grandmother has their wax figures somewhere in the museum."

"Yes, Grandma Rita loved the 1920s," Kimmie shared with interest, pointing to part of the building way past the restroom sign. "There's an entire room dedicated to that era in a side room off one of the far back corners. This place is like a maze. It seems like I find something new every time I walk around this palace."

Told you. 1920s.

"Is the entire place open for us to walk around and see everything?" I asked, sharing an innocent look with Liam. It was also my way of telling Leo that I was going to find a way to locate Norman Palmer's wallet, and nothing he said or did would change my mind. "I haven't had time to stop in before now, and I would love a chance to see all the historic figures."

I will relieve myself on the nearest chest tray for everyone here to see if you so much as step one toe out of the main room.

Don't worry.

Leo wouldn't dare do such a horrible thing.

He was against anyone outside the coven knowing about our family history of our gifts.

You're the one who broke that rule, remember?

"Oh, yes. Feel free to look around." Kimmie smiled at someone over my shoulder. "I'll be sure to stop by the tea shop for more points of interest before next weekend. And thank you, Liam. I'll make reservations at The Back Room for me and my friend. I'm sure it'll be a hit."

Liam and I both stepped aside to allow the group of people behind us to check in their coats. They all looked vaguely familiar, but I don't believe that they've been by the shop.

Even though Liam and I had been talking outside in his vehicle, we were right on time for the festivities. The social hour was just getting into full swing before dancing kicked off.

Honestly, I was surprised that Heidi hadn't been near the front entrance when we arrived.

Surprised? Why would you be surprised when the two of you decided to become the Hardy Boys' twin sisters during your three-hour bathroom ritual getting ready for tonight? Heidi's probably already crawling around on her hands and knees searching for that wallet after being disappointed by Inspector Gadget's repartee.

I usually didn't allow Leo's concern to worry me too much. He was rather dramatic when it came to investigations like these, but he was causing me to wonder if Heidi hadn't shared certain unfortunate details with Detective Swanson.

I can't breathe. Maybe I do have stress-induced asthma. Where is my pipe? Oh, that's right. Back at the house, where you and Heidi should be!

Heidi sharing with Jack that I was looking into an old murder was one thing, but telling him that Norman Palmer's wallet might be found somewhere inside the wax museum was something else entirely.

Is it getting hot in here? It is, isn't it? I need some champagne.

No, it wasn't warm in here, but I understood what Leo meant.

"Do you still need to use the restroom?"

"Yes, please," I blurted out, tucking my purse underneath my arm. I needed a private moment with Leo so that we could sort out the plans for this evening. At the rate Leo and I were exchanging digs, I wouldn't be able to enjoy my date at all. "Yes, I definitely need to use the restroom."

I want no part of your design to dig up the past, which is why I'm here—to protest. Not to help in any way. Put down the shovel, Raven. Right now. I can't believe I'm saying this, but go ahead and enjoy an evening with good ol' Barney Fife. If it will keep you out of trouble, then I'm all for it.

"I asked Alison to reserve us a table near the back," Liam informed me, nodding a greeting toward someone who'd called out his name. A private table away from the larger group tables? I was looking forward to spending more quality time with Liam. Once I found Norman Palmer's wallet, I promised myself that I would focus solely on getting to know Liam. "I'll grab us some drinks and meet you over there."

I nodded my agreement as I took a step in the direction of the restroom. By the time I'd made it halfway across the room,

I was breathing a little bit easier. A few people said hello to me, but I was able to continue my short journey to my destination.

Throngs of people were clustered in groups, allowing me to carefully scan the guests in attendance without having to engage with them just yet.

Monty and his wife were talking with Otis and Karen, while Pearl and Henry were laughing at something Albert had just said. Eugene was nowhere to be found, but Oliver Bend was talking to Mayor Sanders. They were probably engaged in business talk regarding the town's finances and future projects for the New Year.

You know, Eugene might be a tad bit smarter than the others. Maybe he stayed home.

Leo was definitely trying to give me a hint, but it was easier to overlook the obvious. By the time I reached the restroom, something struck me as odd.

Well, not really odd. Out of place.

This New Year's Eve bash was strangely like being back in high school. There were various cliques that I was able to distinguish amongst the guests, even though I'd only lived in Paramour Bay for a little over two months.

Beverly Garber, Justine Davis, and Alison Bend were huddled together, no doubt waiting for Cora's fashionably late entrance. Their husbands weren't standing too far away, lost in their own discussion.

On the other side of the room were Candy Hamilton, Dee Fairuza, Abbie Butterball, and Gillian Reilly. Oh, and Gillian was pregnant with twins, in case you didn't read the last edition of our Paramour Bay series.

You just had to bring up the time when you almost got us killed, didn't you? We can't spend a nice night out without you bringing up death and destruction.

Eileen Weepler and her husband were walking over to join Otis, Monty, and both their wives. Gone was the ugly Christmas sweater in favor of...was that a disco ball on the front of her blouse?

You have to ask?

There were quite a few more people who I recognized, but I couldn't name them all. Plus, I'd finally reached the restroom.

I'm not going in there. I do have a sense of etiquette, you know.

"Oh yes, you are going in there, even if I have to drag you," I mumbled with determination, hitting the door with a little more force than necessary. The door didn't have a handle, but instead one of those gold plates screwed into the wood to signify that it needed to be pushed open. Unfortunately, that meant I might not get the privacy I sought. Thankfully, after a quick check in both stalls, I finally had my moment to lay down the law. "Leo, show yourself right this minute."

Leo's plump furry body suddenly appeared next to the sink.

He grimaced, showing the one fang that was slightly crooked. He lifted his right paw to avoid a bit of water that had obviously been left by someone washing their hands.

Disgusting. You humans live like wild animals.

"Oh, it's clean water," I scolded before leaning against the door to prevent someone from swinging it open. If anyone tried to enter, I'd make up some excuse as to why I was blocking the entrance. "Sit your behind down. Leo, you're ruining my date."

Me? You're the one playing amateur detective again. This is all on you, little miss.

"I'm going to find Norman Palmer's wallet first thing so that I can enjoy the rest of my evening with Liam. We're going to count down the hours and minutes until the ball drops, and then we're going to ring in the New Year together." There. I'd put a plan into place. I was feeling better already, and now all I had to do was see it through. "There is nothing you need to worry about, Leo, so you should go on home and spend the evening with Ted talking about old times together. I'm worried about him."

You should be.

"I know Ted is worried that the townsfolk believe Nan killed Norman Palmer. Once I prove that she didn't have anything to do with his murder, Ted will feel better."

Ted's not going to feel better until you stop searching for answers, because there's a chance he'll end up...dead like Fred.

Eleven

"LEO, GET BACK HERE RIGHT NOW," I whispered forcefully, not wanting anyone hanging outside of the bathroom to hear me and assume I was talking to myself. Everyone already thought the Marigolds were a little off their rockers, and I certainly didn't want to confirm their suspicions. "Leo?"

I called out to him four more times, but all I got in return was continued silence.

Fudgsicles and Pop-Tarts.

Leo was trying to prove his point, and now I was left to my own devices.

Fine.

He could stuff his pipe and smoke it.

If that's the way Leo wanted to play this game, then I would continue with the plan Heidi and I had put into place from the onset—find Norman Palmer's wallet before ringing in the New Year with our dates.

I took a brief second to look into the mirror to make sure my lipstick hadn't smeared before smoothing a loose strand of black hair back into place. With a quick brush of the counter with a paper towel to wipe away any evidence of Leo's presence, I was good to go.

"Oh! I'm so sorry," I exclaimed to the person I bumped into after opening the restroom door. I instinctively laid a hand on the man's arm in regret. "I should have been watching where I was—"

"It's fine," Rye murmured, his dark penetrating gaze practically cutting right through me. I know what you're thinking, but I wasn't talking about that kind of attraction. It was much more intense than that. Almost as if he knew what I was up to and maybe even my true identity as a witch. I tried unsuccessfully to swallow around the lump in my throat. "I shouldn't have been standing so close to the entrance of the restroom."

I leave you alone for one second. One second, Raven.

I'd first met Rye at the inn, where he'd helped Gertie get rid of a tree branch that had crashed through one of the upstairs bedrooms during a storm. Leo had been wary upon first sight of the handyman, and I tended to trust Leo's first impressions.

Don't panic. I can knock over one of those centerpieces, catch the tablecloth on fire, and get you out of this.

I do know what you're wondering.

The readers are wondering why you're still standing in front of an overtly dangerous man and not considering my wise offer to create a distraction.

No, you're wondering what's the difference between Leo's theatrics over a wallet and his warning about Rye. Well, they're two distinctly different things.

No, they're not.

Nothing that happened fifty-three years ago could be an imminent danger to me or Heidi.

Have I taught you nothing? Time is so relative to some

beings. Not everything that goes bump in the night is benevolent. Sometimes running away to fight another day is the better part of valor. Discretion is quite preferable to rash bravery that gets your fur set on fire.

Speaking of Heidi, she'd thought Rye was rather mysterious—in a good way. The old saying tall, dark, and handsome might just come into play, as well.

Excuse me? Apparently, you aren't much of a student of Heidi's taste in men. Patrick, Jack Swanson, and this handyman? Hmph. She'd have better luck sticking with cats. There's a reason most old ladies end up with multiple cats, you know.

"We didn't get to formally meet before," Rye continued, his sole focus on me as he held out his hand. "Rye Dolgiram."

"Yes, it's nice to meet you. Gertie speaks very highly of your skills," I praised before shaking his hand. I guess it wasn't very nice of me to concentrate on the center of my palm, fully expecting the warmth to appear as a sign of warning. A little tingle that Rye wasn't what he pretended to be in the way of confirming Leo's suspicions would have been nice, but I got nothing. Instead, the only heat I experienced was from his room-temperature fingers as they wrapped around the back of my hand. "My name is Raven—"

Oh, thank you, supernatural beings of all sorts. Heidi is here to save the day.

"I've been looking all over for you," Heidi exclaimed excitedly, cutting off my introduction to Rye and explaining Leo's comment. She brushed the curls from her face as she continued. "I think I've found—"

"Heidi, you remember Rye, don't you?" I asked, making sure Heidi didn't get to finish her sentence. I had a pretty good idea of what she was talking about, but it turned out I didn't have to worry about her slipping up and revealing what we were really up to. From the arch of her right eyebrow, it was clear that she quickly figured out who was standing in front of me. "We were just making proper introductions."

An introduction I advised against, I want to point out for later scrutiny.

"Heidi Connolly," she said with a weirdly apologetic smile. Well, she *was* on a date with Jack Swanson, after all. "I hope you don't mind, but I've got to steal Raven for the time being."

Heidi's timing is perfection, as always. She seems to just glow tonight, doesn't she? Did I mention to you that she might be my soulmate?

Without another word, Heidi latched onto my wrist and began to drag me through the throngs of people who seemed to have multiplied several-fold since my short visit to the restroom. Only one thing stuck out the most—Jack must have really impressed Heidi for my best friend forever to not give Rye more than a passing moment of her time.

"Did you find the elusive wallet?" It was the only explanation as to why Heidi was in such a hurry. There must have been something inside the billfold that answered all of our questions. "What was inside? Did you find the reason *he* was in Paramour Bay?"

Tell me she didn't find it. Tell me she didn't destroy my idea of the perfect woman. Tell me she didn't spear me through the heart. Tell me she didn't find it.

I didn't want to call Norman Palmer by his name or someone might overhear and become suspicious of our activities, but Leo chanting that mantra in my head over and over was liable to have me blurting something highly inappropriate out loud.

All you have to do is tell me that you'll leave well enough alone. I'll go on home and even share a pipeful of catnip with Ted. I'll even teach him how to blow smoke rings.

"Wallet?" Heidi finally turned on her high heels in a flash that would have had me breaking my ankle six ways to Sunday. She waved away the word as if it meant nothing whatsoever. "Oh, that. No, not yet. Raven, I think I've found my soulmate. Seriously, Jack is the complete package, and I do mean complete. Did you know that he asked the bartender if he could get behind the bar for just a moment to create the most delicious drink I've ever tasted in my life? I mean, he even put on a little show with twirling bottles that had everyone's attention riveted to my date."

Soulmate? How could everything have gone so wrong so quickly?

I'd been so caught up in trying to figure out a way to locate Norman Palmer's wallet that I almost forgot the reason we were here celebrating in the first place.

No. No. No. I've changed my mind. You need to get Heidi away from Jack. We have a new mission. If that means searching for the devil's missing pitchfork, so be it. Let's go!

"Heidi, lead the way," I said, casting a quick glance at the ball. It hadn't even moved an inch. It was still relatively early, and we had all evening to tour the museum in search of Norman Palmer's wallet. I needed to slow-play my plan. "I'd love to try that drink."

How can you drink at a time like this? All hands on deck! Loose lips sink ships!

Heidi's bright smile was all the encouragement I needed to take a little time for myself. Before long, we were both standing in front of a reserved bar-height table in the back supplied with premium New Year's Eve hats for the men, tiaras for the ladies, paper blowers, and confetti...and four colorful layered drinks with decorative umbrellas.

"Welcome back," Liam greeted me with a searching gaze. Once he noticed my smile, his shoulders relaxed some. He then stood and pulled out the tall bar chair next to him, which I gladly took. I used the small strap of my clutch to hang on the corner of my chair inbound toward my date. "It seems Jack here used to bartend for a while back in the day."

"It's been years, but I still remember a few tricks of the trade."

For the next hour, small talk was had between the four of us regarding movies, television shows, hobbies, life in the city, and the collection of odd jobs we'd all had in our past lives. We ate, drank, laughed, and shared stories in a way that wasn't awkward like some of the rather disappointing first dates I'd experienced.

I'd been so worried about our first date being with the entire town, only to discover that we had our own private oasis at one of the few reserved tables. We could also observe the inner ring of group tables circling the dance floor. It was a perfect place to be on a perfect night.

In all honesty, it was the most relaxing sixty minutes I've had since moving to Paramour Bay.

Interestingly enough, Leo had left me to enjoy the evening. I hoped he'd gone home to be with Ted and enjoy a nice, relaxing night in peace.

I've just been waiting patiently for the inevitable explosion.

I paused, holding the drink I'd been about to take another sip of against my bottom lip. Leo didn't say another word, so I held the little umbrella to the side and tilted the glass. It gave me a bit of cover to look around to make sure Leo hadn't forgotten what he was doing here and make an appearance.

The alcoholic beverage got stuck in my throat when my eyes landed on the bomb.

Oh, trust me. It's not as impossible as you might think.

"Raven, are you okay?" Liam scooted his chair away from the table a bit so that he could pat me on the back. I'd really sucked in a lungful, so it wasn't a surprise when a tear ran down my face in my struggle to regain the ability to breathe. "Slow and steady."

I held up my hand and nodded my head in an effort to let Liam, Jack, and Heidi know that I was still alive. It took another minute or two to eventually clear my airway, and by then...well, no. I still hadn't accepted what had been right there next to me the entire evening.

"Sorry about that," I managed to croak, since my voice was now rather hoarse. "I'm fine."

Keep telling yourself that, sweetheart.

"Wrong tube," I explained, using my napkin to dab the side of my left eye. I even gave a weak smile to back up my odd behavior. "I'm all good now."

Liam was now rubbing my back in sympathy, but nothing anyone said or did could make what I saw unseen.

Nothing. Nada. Zilch.

I so understood why Leo hadn't wanted me to come to the wax museum tonight. This entire time, I'd thought it had to do with Norman Palmer. It had nothing to do with the man's murder and everything to do with—

Maybe next time you'll listen to those who know better.

The palm of my hand had literally become so hot that I almost panicked.

Almost.

I recovered quickly by grabbing onto my drink, using the

condensation on the glass to cool my heated flesh, hoping steam wouldn't rise.

Were you going to throw an energy ball at me?

The incredulity in Leo's voice would have been laughable in any other situation than the one I'd found myself in. I'd handled a lot in the past two months—moving to a small town, leaving my mom and best friend behind, discovering I'm a witch, accepting that I could talk to a cat, and learning there was more to this life on a supernatural plane than I'd ever imagined.

I'd thought I was taking it all in stride and handling it quite well.

Well, I guess when you put it that way, I should give you some credit.

Thankfully, Heidi was able to get the conversation flowing again. Once Liam began to tell a story of the time he'd needed to employ the Heimlich maneuver while in the police academy, I was able to catch Heidi's attention.

I'm not so sure that's a good idea. As you just pointed out, you've taken this new life of yours in stride. I should have given you a bit more credit. I absolutely should have, but do you remember Heidi's first initial reaction? There was nothing agile or accepting about that moment.

Leo did make a good point, but this wasn't something I could keep to myself. At first, I shifted my eyes to the right in hopes she'd look in the direction of the framed picture on the wall. All that got me was a tilt of Heidi's curls as she tried to make out what I was trying to convey.

You still have time to remain silent. Even criminals are given that right, you know.

It looked as if I'd have to resort to jerking my head to the side in hopes that she'd finally see the photograph. From the look of horror that spread across her face after setting eyes on what had prompted my choking spree, it was a surefire bet that she'd finally seen what had me sucking down my drink with my lungs.

I didn't know human lips could contort like that.

Neither had I, and panic began to rise up in my chest at Heidi's look of terror.

You better do something quick.

Don't get me wrong. I figured Heidi's response would go one way or another. Such as her trying to get the men to leave the table so that we could discuss what I'd discovered in private. Or maybe discreetly excusing us to use the restroom, where we could then talk over such a shocking discovery.

Wow, were you way off the mark on that one or what? Maybe you shouldn't mix alcohol with witchcraft, Sabrina.

Heidi jumped to her feet so fast that the table tipped in Liam's and my direction.

Oh, this isn't going to work out well for anyone. Abandon ship!

Liam stopped mid-story to try and prevent our glasses from tipping over into our laps, but there was no stopping the scream that tore forth from Heidi's throat. She could rival any scream queen from back in the day of B-list horror movies.

I didn't blame her, really.

You see, the framed photograph on the wall beside us was obviously taken in this same museum many years ago based on its apparent age. It depicted several wax figures from that day. The picture itself was black and white, worn from old age, and practically came across as a vintage tintype photograph. I realize that it was more modern than the 1920s, but there was one individual who most certainly couldn't have been made of wax.

Yet there he stood, suit and all—Ted.

He looked good as a wax figure, didn't he? Very dapper, indeed.

I did the only thing I could, given the circumstances of Heidi's reaction...I piled on.

"Spider!"

Twelve

"I THINK I need one of those paper bag thingies," Heidi wheezed as she clutched her throat. She was leaning up against the restroom wall with her head tilted back, looking as if she'd run a couple of miles in those black heels. "Please tell me that picture wasn't real. It was Photoshopped, right? Ted isn't like a thousand years old, is he?"

We don't have time for this. Basic math skills and a fourth-grade science teacher should just about get us there from here. Can't you just throw a bucket of cold water on her?

"Who was that in the picture, Leo?" I demanded to know, dealing somewhat better than Heidi with this current predicament we found ourselves in. "Please tell me that wasn't really... Ted. I mean, it did look like him, but then again, it didn't. I don't know how to explain it other than I *know* it was him."

Then why ask me if you already know the answer? Hmmm, it still hasn't sunk in for you, has it? There's no easy way to put this, so I'll just blurt it out—Ted is a golem. A golem is a protective servant of the spell caster or what was called by some a

Tallowheart Golem, in antiquity, since that is how they rendered candles.

"A what?"

Well, Ted's not actually a true golem, per se.

"Golem?"

Yeah, those creepy things made of clay or rock. Rosemary mixed the golem enchantment with an anthropomorphism incantation to bring Ted to life from an existing wax figure. She did an exceptionally fine job, too. With the exception of his teeth. Oh, and his inability to string together two sentences without a half an hour's preparation. He started out kind of rough, but he's come a long way in ten years, wouldn't you say?

"Anthro-what?"

Leo was once again sitting on the sink, though this time he was watching Heidi very closely to ensure she didn't hyperventilate and pass out.

Is she turning blue? I think she's turning blue.

"Raven, tell me what is going on," Heidi demanded as she pointed a trembling finger toward the door. "Was that a wax figure of Ted or was that *Ted* Ted?"

"*Ted* Ted. I think."

It could have been worse, right? I mean, there had been a time when I'd thought Ted was a zombie. A golem is much better, if one looks at it that way.

"Heidi, you're going to have to pull it together and—"

Leo was squinting his eyes with his mouth wide open as he made an awful noise, but I'd gotten used to the sound of his laughter.

"This isn't funny, Leo." How in creation had no one in this town made the connection before? How had Alison not recognized Ted from the picture? Granted, there were a couple of different oddities between the wax figure in the photo and the man—well, golem—himself. With that said, why bring a wax figure to life that someone could recognize? A little risky, don't you think? Personally, I believe a body from a grave a town or two over from the 1800s would have been a much safer bet. I didn't even want to contemplate that thinking about resurrection spells had become my new reality. "You're always warning me not to take risks, and what do you know? Nan goes and brings a wax figure to life as if no one will notice Ted's resemblance to a missing wax statue—"

Heidi gasped, which promptly had me believing she was about to drop dead from lack of oxygen to her brain. Thankfully, my rant to Leo seemed to have shocked her out of her daze. She started wagging a finger in my direction.

"It all makes sense now!" Heidi grabbed the sink as she practically came nose to nose with Leo, whose right eye was now almost as big as his left. "The missing wax figure! Alison Bend mentioned that a wax figure in storage had been missing for years. It was Ted all along!"

"Ow!" I had once again been leaning up against the door to prevent anyone from walking in on us talking to Leo. I must have inadvertently taken a step forward while Heidi was connecting the dots. The back of my head wouldn't have a bump, but the thud against my scalp still hurt. "Trixie!"

I'd only ever seen Trixie Fredericks, the owner of the only diner in town, a handful of times. The older woman was rather short with white hair, but she seemed to get around okay given that she was in her late seventies. Truthfully, I was surprised to see her in attendance tonight.

I was standing directly in her path, though, motioning with my hand behind my back that Leo needed to vanish. Hopefully, his short-term memory hadn't kicked in. His presence was the last thing Heidi and I needed to explain after the spider fiasco that Liam and Jack were probably still talking about. Between the two of us, we'd shoved the table back and forth a dozen times battling an imaginary spider.

I've begun taking huperzine. I can't remember if it's doing any good. Did you know that the herb-like substance comes from a plant called Chinese club moss? You should try it sometime. Hey, maybe I should smoke it.

"Raven, dear. Is your friend okay?" Trixie asked, trying to shuffle around me to get a better look at Heidi. I was afraid to move too soon, but I didn't want to appear rude. "Everyone is talking about that huge spider that dropped down from the ceiling. Horrible, I tell you. Alison needs to have a talk with the cleaning crew that comes in here every Sunday night or maybe she should call an exterminator."

It's amazing what people will believe with the slightest suggestion.

"I'm quite alright, Ms. Fredericks," Heidi said after clearing her throat. It was her way of telling me that Leo had vanished into thin air. His departure certainly hadn't stopped him from chiming in with his two cents, though. I cautiously shifted, not sure that Leo wouldn't magically reappear and create another mess I wasn't so sure I could clean up this time. "Phobias can be tricky little devils, can't they?"

"Oh, you should see me with snakes," Trixie replied, brushing past me to stand in front of Heidi. The scent of baby powder was overwhelming. "I'm deathly afraid of them. Well, you should know that Alison was able to get your table put back together with a clean tablecloth and new tableware. Just don't lean on it too hard. I don't think it will survive another round."

Heidi continued to reassure Trixie that all was okay and

that we would be returning to our dates shortly. I can only imagine what Liam and Jack thought of us—screaming like the dead had risen from the grave.

Theoretically, you wouldn't be far off with that theory. Regardless, it's still technically wrong.

I'm sure my expression looked much like Heidi's when she'd discovered Ted in the framed photograph, but Leo's voice had me glancing at the sink. You see, some of Leo's orange and black fur remained behind in a couple of tufts that couldn't possibly be missed. Unless, of course, Trixie's eyesight was as bad as his memory.

Are you actually wishing cataracts on an old woman? Wow. First, you were going to blow me to smithereens with an energy ball, and now this. You're falling apart at the seams, Raven. You need to get a firm grip.

"Trixie, that was so sweet of you to check on Heidi," I exclaimed, hoping to draw Trixie's attention toward me. If I could get around the two of them, I'd be able to quickly wipe away any trace of Leo from the restroom. "I'll just wash my hands and then we can—"

I cringed when Trixie's gasp echoed off the restroom walls. Sure enough, she'd caught sight of Leo's tufts of fur stuck to the counter.

"Disgusting," Trixie muttered, reaching for the paper towel dispenser. "Cora is constantly leaving behind remnants of that fake fur wrap of hers. You'd think she'd have the decency to clean up after herself. She's worse than my cat."

Don't you dare do it.

Leo's warning came a little too late. The mere mention of Cora reminded me why I was investigating Norman Palmer's murder to begin with, which was to clear Nan's name.

What better way than to question the original individuals who'd given statements in regard to Norman Palmer during his tenure here in Paramour Bay? After all, the killer was still out there. Who was to say that particular someone wasn't in attendance at this New Year's Eve bash?

Now you're accusing an old lady of murder? That's pretty low, even for the Hardy Sisters.

I wasn't doing anything of the sort, but it had crossed my mind that Trixie Fredericks would have only been in her mid to late twenties at the time of the murder. She and Norman had supposedly gotten into an argument over something inane, but could there have been something more to their disagreement?

"Trixie, do you remember Norman Palmer?" I walked over to the sink where Heidi had moved to the side, her blue eyes widening once she recognized my plan. "Cora brought up the old murder, saying that her behavior over the story was the reason she and my mother no longer get along."

Trixie had used a paper towel out of the black dispenser to wipe up the cat hairs that Leo had left behind. I'm not so sure what she would have thought had Cora not been wearing her prized wrap.

"Oh, dear. That was a very long time ago," Trixie declared, frowning as if I'd brought up unpleasant memories. I guess I had, but it wasn't as if she'd known the man personally. Had she? "I do regret the way I handled Mr. Palmer's complaint. You see, I had just opened up the diner. I'd used breakfast as a trial run, and that particular week was when I'd extended the hours to include lunch and dinner. I hadn't counted on the crowd, so we were a little understaffed at first. Mr. Palmer's meal had inadvertently gotten moved to the side, and it was rather cold by the time his waitress served him. As I said, I was young and inexperienced. I certainly hadn't handled the situation as well as I should have. And then to find out that he…"

Trixie's voice—not as frail as you might think—trailed off as she became lost in the past.

Heidi nudged me on the arm to do something, so I quickly washed my hands and gestured toward the paper towel device attached to the wall.

"I can only imagine what a shock it was to the residents to learn of Mr. Palmer's death." I took the proffered towel and dried my hands while I tried a different approach, and one that might actually pay off. "You don't believe that someone from Paramour Bay had anything to do with Mr. Palmer's death, do you?"

Trixie's mother must have named her that for her disposition, because the older woman was rather spry. Her go-get-'em attitude was rather infectious as she leaned in close, like we weren't the only three in the closed-off space and someone was bound to overhear her secrets. She even motioned for Heidi to come closer, so that all three of us were huddled together in front of the sink.

"I always believed that Albert had something to do with it," Trixie whispered as if we were conspiring against the man. "I've never seen Albert get so red in the face as the day Mr. Palmer ran over those rosebushes. Most likely, Albert would have gotten off on temporary insanity. He's always been quick in the temper department."

It was too late to move when the door suddenly swung open, revealing Candy, Dee, and Gillian. Music, laughter, and conversation from the main area drifted in with them, and it was a stark reminder that our dates were waiting for our return…and no doubt wondering if we'd lost our minds.

"Heidi, are you okay?" Candy asked the moment she laid

eyes on us. Her reddish-orange hair was styled to perfection with most likely a touch of product from her salon. "It must have been horrible to have that spider fall from the ceiling onto your table. How you didn't run through a wall is beyond me. I would have died dead as a doornail, right on the spot. Arachnophobia is nothing to sneeze at. I'm the kind of person who would burn a house down to get rid of one."

"I'm better now," Heidi exclaimed, fanning herself in a dramatic air. She was a better actress than me, which got me thinking that Leo hadn't piped in his two cents in quite a while. He was usually the first one to praise her. "Eileen said she saw the spider and that it was bigger than her hand."

I wasn't too sure what to think of that statement. There hadn't been a spider at all, but I guess the hive mentality had kicked in when I began whacking the tablecloth with one of the boys' party hats and shoving the table back at Heidi.

"Gotta pee, gotta pee," Gillian announced in a sing-song tone, pushing past Candy and Dee. She gave all of us an apologetic smile as she made a beeline for the second stall. "They tell me it's only going to get worse once I hit the third trimester. I'm going to need diapers before either of these two will. Either that or you'll see me dragging a porta-potty behind me down River Bay."

Everyone began to gush over the fact that Gillian was pregnant with twins, even me, until Trixie pulled at the sleeve of my blouse. She had a contemplative look in those wise eyes of hers. That alone should have warned me that she had more to say on the subject of Norman Palmer, but I certainly hadn't prepared myself for something so shocking.

"Rita let it slip years later that she never caught a plane to England that year. Rumor had it that she was carrying on some sordid tryst with an electrician over near Hartford." Trixie patted my arm in a palliative nature. The reassuring gesture missed its mark by a mile. "By that time, everyone had moved on. Rita was a sweet woman who wouldn't even harm a fly. Same as your grandmother. I guess I never thought about it, but maybe that's why this museum has spiders—Alison must take after her mother. You can never tell about the quiet ones."

Thirteen

"HEIDI, Rita Carter could have been the one to murder Norman Palmer," I whispered in incredulity as we weaved in and out of the throngs of people surrounding the dance floor. "She was in the state of Connecticut the entire time. This changes the whole ball game. I need to tell Liam this so that he can officially reopen the investigation."

The ball had dropped a smidgen, telling me that there were still a couple of hours before midnight. We would have time to search for Norman Palmer's wallet while convincing Liam that he should—

"In case you forgot, Rita Carter is long gone," Heidi murmured as she steered us around another group of partygoers. "Unless the woman managed to blurt out a confession on her deathbed, it's unlikely that Liam would find any evidence to support reopening a long-dead cold case. And might I just add that I'm still in shock over discovering that Ted is a...what did Leo call him?"

"A sort of wax golem and something else I can't exactly remember."

It's good to know I'm not the only one with short-term memory loss, but what the hey...the gang's all here.

Leo picked a fine time to rejoin the party, and probably on purpose. How was I supposed to bombard him with questions about Rita Carter when I was currently surrounded by practically everyone in town?

Elsie and Wilma are the smart ones. They stayed home. They're currently in their dressing gowns, commiserating over Dick Clark's untimely death. Wilma met him in person one time, you know. I didn't know Dick as well as I knew Frank Sinatra, though.

"We'll go with golem," Heidi decided, making it easier on us. She grabbed a champagne glass off one of the stations as we continued to make our way toward the table we'd destroyed in front of our dates. The slight tremor in her hand told me that she wasn't over such a shocking discovery as easily as it had appeared. "There's not enough alcohol in this room to steady my nerves. Witchcraft is one thing. You know, casting spells to find lost items. But to bring to life a...I can't even go there. I mean, did you see Ted in that picture? Holy cow. Granted, he looked better in the picture. And taller, if that's possible."

Heidi lifted the fine crystal to her lips and drank half the glass in one sip. I couldn't really blame her, but I was personally going to switch to coffee without anyone being the wiser. Liam promised me he'd figure out a way to obtain my life source, and I trusted him. More alcohol was the last thing I needed right now.

Humans. I'll never understand you. Since when is a wax figure brought to life more frightening than a half-rotten zombie crawling out of a grave somewhere? You people never cease to amaze me.

I guess when Leo put it like that, we might have overreacted a tad bit.

And would the two of you stop talking about witchcraft out in the open? You're making me lose more fur by the pound. At this rate, I'll end up like Larry.

Larry Butterball used to be Nan's attorney, so I guess you could say he was mine now. He was divorced from Abbie and currently dating Mindy. Oh, and he's bald.

"Heidi, focus," I directed, taking the champagne from her hand and setting it down on an empty tray that was positioned on another station. She was quick to react, but she always settled down and did what needed to be done. Plus, she was one of the most intelligent women I had ever met. "Rita never flew to England. If she let that detail slip to Trixie, what else could she have said that would shed new light on the details of the case?"

"Like confessing to committing a murder to a local newspaper reporter?"

When Heidi put it like that, I guess I was reaching.

"It still needs to be investigated."

No, it doesn't. It needs to be left dead and buried.

The fact that Leo was still arguing about the case told me that I was bound to discover more than just Ted's origin. That alone should have given me second thoughts, but clearing Nan's name was more important than whatever else she'd done back then.

I wouldn't bet the farm.

"You should do another spell."

Oh, that's a stunning idea. She's certainly batting a thousand tonight.

"Nothing seems to work," I reminded Heidi, recalling the blackness I saw every time an incantation was used. Yes, the locater spell eventually worked, but what was with the wavering blackness? It had to be the lake water. There was no other answer. "Let me handle this."

Like you handled the spider fiasco? I wonder what the limit is on their property damage claim for this place.

"I improvised," I muttered under my breath before pasting a smile on my face.

We'd reached our table, and both Liam and Jack stood from their respective high-backed barstools. Liam returned my smile with the most charming grin and held up what was sure to be...tea?

He'd never make it as a barista, would he? Time to call it a night.

Was that a string hanging over the side of the cup?

It sure isn't a coffee bean baggie soaking in there.

"Thank you, Liam," I replied, hoping I'd been able to keep the disappointment out of my voice. I'm pretty sure I failed miserably. "I needed something warm."

Heidi began to apologize profusely for causing such a scene, but Jack handled the situation perfectly by comparing his fear of heights to her fear of spiders. As we all settled back down in our seats, he told the story of chasing a suspect out onto the roof of a building and how the suspect had jumped from one rooftop to another as if he had wings attached to his ankles. Jack's partner immediately followed, and Jack stopped on a dime.

"...and there I stood, looking down eighteen stories to the ground below. I froze. Couldn't move a muscle. I'm still living that one down to this day."

You should tell Heidi that I'm not afraid of heights. I can jump from one counter to another with ease. I bet Jack couldn't land on both of his legs. That's a plus for me—agile as a panther.

"Did you really think that I wouldn't follow through?" Liam asked, leaning in close so that no one could hear our conversation. His warmth immediately invaded my space as he nodded toward the cup still in my hand. "Go ahead. Taste your tea."

I arched my left eyebrow as I brought the warm cup to my lips, amazed that I'd missed the delicious aroma rising from the dark black beverage steaming away in my hand.

Heaven in a cup.

At least, that was the first description that crossed my mind. I'm pretty sure it had a lot to do with the man who'd brought it to me, as well.

"I stole one of the strings with the labels on it from the box of teas Alison had at one of the stations to make your beverage look like tea. Now don't go telling anyone," Liam warned with a wink. "I am the sheriff, after all."

Guilt immediately flooded my system.

I trusted him, yet how could he do the same when I was lying by omission? My confession bubbled up inside of me.

"Liam, there's something that you should—"

A loud crash came from the dance area, cutting off my admission. It was instinct to stand up from the table and rush over to make sure no one was hurt. We technically followed Liam's lead, because he'd threaded through the guests like the professional he was until he'd reached his destination.

I hope you're happy.

"Cora, are you alright?"

Oh, this was bad.

This was really bad.

There was no doubt that Leo had something to do with the frosting currently sliding down Cora's cheek and onto her faux fur coat. To say that she was a sight was an understatement as her mouth was formed in a perfect O and her left eye was closed to prevent the white icing from getting into her eye.

What was I supposed to do? Let you announce to the world that you are a witch?

It was a good thing that all the other partygoers had their focus on Cora. I used their inattentiveness on me to allow myself to relieve my pent-up frustration.

"I wasn't going to do any such thing, Leo," I furiously whispered, grabbing Heidi's arm so that anyone nearby would think I was talking to her. "I was going to tell him what Trixie said about Rita Carter. How could you do something like this? Look at the poor woman!"

You were too going to confess! Remember, I can read your thoughts. I had no choice but to throw a slice of cake from the top tier. How was I to know that Cora would be the one in the way?

It was true that my remorse had risen due to the fact that I was keeping such a life-changing secret from Liam, but I would never just blurt out I was a witch with so many people nearby to overhear such a confession.

"Leo did this?" Heidi asked in shock, staying behind with me as Liam and Jack rushed forward to make sure that Cora was okay. Liam was currently using a napkin to wipe the icing from Cora's face while Jack asked one of the servers to bring him a dustpan. "Wow. Leo sure is quick on his feet. I was just going to kick you underneath the table."

"What is with you two? Nobody seems to trust me." Did I come across as completely incompetent? No, don't answer that question. It was time to get to the bottom of this mystery that I'd set out to solve. "Let's go help clean Cora up so that we can look for Norman Palmer's wallet while we're gone."

You might want to rethink that first part. Look who just walked through the door.

"Is that my mother?" I asked in horror, not understanding why times like this didn't go my way. I mean, I accepted the fact that I was a bit accident-prone, but this was beginning to resemble something akin to bad karma. Hadn't I done enough by forgiving Cora? "Why would she show up now?"

I had no choice but to take desperate measures.

This was all Leo's fault.

Fault? I'm looking out for your best interest, dear Raven. A familiar must do what a familiar has gotta do.

My mother stood there looking elegant with her hair swept up to perfection, a beautiful black wraparound dress that tied in the front, and emerald gems to complete the ensemble. She was a stunning woman, and her satisfaction that Cora was now covered in icing was a little too noticeable at the moment.

"Do not panic," Heidi instructed me, though she was a little too late. She blocked my view of Mom as she turned on her high heels to face me. "I'll take care of this. I won't allow your mother to ruin your first date with Liam."

And here I thought you were doing that all on your own.

I wasn't the type to hyperventilate. I wasn't even the type to throw temper tantrums, either. Both were more a Heidi thing, but now I completely understood how someone might reach their breaking point and act out.

My fingertips began to tingle and warmth commenced in the middle of my palm.

Heidi squeezed my heated hand in reassurance before she walked across the dance floor to intervene. I couldn't help but glance up at the large disco ball hanging from the ceiling. I guess Leo's distraction could have been worse.

Alert! Get to higher ground!

Leo's warning came a little too late as I bumped into Albert even before I could head back to the table. He steadied me with his weathered hands, but the expression on his face was anything but reassuring.

Those beady eyes are scarier than mine. You know, that's saying something when I admit that.

"I heard from Mayor Sanders who heard it from Trixie that you're looking into the old Palmer murder." Truthfully, that one sentence was the most Albert had said to me since I'd moved to Paramour Bay. There was a gruff edge to his tone, so I could understand Leo's need to warn me against such an encounter. Could Albert have killed Norman Palmer over a rosebush? "Otis put in some long hours investigating who could have done killed that man. I wasn't fond of Palmer. Neither was Eugene. That's no secret, but Otis never took stock in my opinion that Palmer came here to stir up trouble. He was up to no good. He was always poking around the museum when he shouldn't be. If he wasn't, he was parked on the inn's porch smoking one of his funny cigarettes while keeping an eye on the place. It's a shame that your grandmother got caught up with such a no-good troublemaker."

Pssst. Raven. Hey, Raven.

Leo didn't have to say anything more for me to recognize that his short-term memory loss had kicked in during my conversation with Albert.

Did you know that your mother is here? She just can't let me have a good start to the year, can she? One night out with my girl was all I wanted.

A good start to the year would be clearing the Marigold name of shame.

Is that the reason we're here? What did you do? Better yet, what is your mother going to do?

Was Albert suggesting that Rita Carter killed Norman Palmer? Or my grandmother?

Wait. Rita killed Norman? Ohhhhh. Well, that figures.

Trixie believed that Albert had something to do with the murder, but Albert believed Rita or Nan were the culprit. Several residents still suspected Nan, but only one theory was the correct.

Or all of them are wrong.

Leo's memory had returned, and I know full well he had the answers I was seeking. There was also no doubt in my mind that he'd been the one to drag my mother here tonight.

I have no idea what you're talking about. Aren't you partied out? I know I am. Let's get Heidi and hit the road.

Albert's scenario made more sense than the others, especially if Rita never really caught that plane to England so many years ago. The police just took her whereabouts at face value. They never even asked her if she had anything to do with it.

Many years ago. Exactly. Who cares what happened all those years ago? Now, why don't we go see Regina and have some cake?

Why would Rita allow everyone to think she'd gone on her annual vacation when she'd done the exact opposite and run off to meet up with some guy in Hartford?

Everyone needs some me time. I know I do. How about you?

"Thanks, Albert." His insight into Norman Palmer's behavior had me convinced the man's interest was solely on the museum. Maybe he'd used Nan and the tea shop as a diversion. "Every piece of information helps, and I appreciate you passing this on to me."

"I wish you the best of luck, Raven."

Albert made his way through the guests who were finally departing to their tables after Beverly had escorted Cora to the restroom to help clean off the rest of the icing. A dry napkin could only do so much.

An upbeat music selection began to spill out of the speakers once more.

"Raven Lattice Marigold."

Like nails on a chalkboard. Do you see what I had to resort to? That alone should tell you to leave well enough alone.

"Good evening, Mother," I greeted, turning to find a chagrined Heidi by my mom's side. "Why are you even here? I thought you were spending New Year's Eve with your friends in the city."

"That's exactly where I should be," Regina replied, tilting her head up another fraction to let me know she was annoyed with me. "You know who had to let me know that you won't leave well enough alone."

I'm relegated to you know who? I take it back, Regina. Go home. I can handle this without your pleasant personality.

To my mother's credit, she didn't react to Leo's response. She'd had a little more practice in the witchcraft department than me, but that didn't mean she was right to ignore the stain on our surname.

"Mom, I'm on a date. Please don't ruin this night for me."

You did that all on your own, Sherlock.

"Technically, we're both on dates," Heidi tossed into the conversation. Her blue gaze landed somewhere behind me. "And speaking of which, they're coming our way. 'Night."

Heidi makes a great Watson, doesn't she? Effortless.

Leo was having too much fun this evening, and I'd figured out why. He'd purposefully been throwing a wrench into my date ever since we left the house. He'd seen to it that Cora was covered in icing from head to toe, and he'd brought my mother to town all to keep me so occupied that I hadn't had time to locate Norman Palmer's wallet.

A familiar must do what a familiar must do, Raven.

"Mom, why don't you go help out Cora while Heidi and I have Jack and Liam take us on a tour of the wax museum?" I said, making sure that my voice was loud enough to be heard. Granted, I'd thought about the fact that my mother was more than likely more powerful than I was at the moment, but I wasn't too worried about a fireworks display in the middle of the town's big New Year's Eve gala. She'd left behind this life close to thirty-five years ago. "I'm sure after all this time you'll let bygones be bygones, right? Oh, and by the way—I just signed a three-year lease for the tea shop. Happy New Year."

Oh, that was cold.

Fourteen

"IS THERE something happening between you and your mother that I should be aware of?" Liam asked warily as we finally walked out of the main room. I matched his casual pace, enjoying this time with him. Heidi and Jack had gone on ahead, giving Liam and me some much-needed privacy. "I wasn't aware she was attending the party this evening."

Liam had stated the obvious so diplomatically that I couldn't help but laugh.

"I'm sorry. I truly am," I professed, wishing I didn't have to bend the truth. It wasn't fair, and I would eventually have to figure out a way to right this wrong. "I didn't know she'd be here, either. Mom wasn't too thrilled when I told her I was looking into the old Palmer murder."

"I can understand how she might feel that way." Liam was being too gracious, in my opinion. "The guilty party is still out there, and it's never wise to stir up a hornet's nest."

He's brighter than I thought he was. Not by much, but he's showing promise.

Leo was still lurking around, but I wasn't going to

acknowledge his presence. I might have actually had a chance to solve Norman Palmer's murder by now if it wasn't for Leo.

Some things are better left dead and buried.

So Leo kept saying. It made me wonder why he'd want to cover up these developments after everything I'd discovered thus far.

The room to the right of the main party consisted of just what Otis had said it would—famous crooners from back in the day. There was good ol' Frank Sinatra, Dean Martin, Nat King Cole, Tony Bennett, and many more staged around pianos, microphones, and underneath muted stage lights on various stages around the room.

"What kind of music do you like?" I asked Liam, not wanting to talk about the case or my family history. Don't get me wrong, I was still keeping a lookout for the red silk I'd identified as the material camouflaging Norman Palmer's lost wallet, but I was truly enjoying this time alone with Liam. "I like a fairly eclectic mixture. I guess it depends on my mood— pop, classic rock, country. You name it, I'll listen to it."

"I'm pretty much the same," Liam admitted, stopping in front of Frank Sinatra's wax figure. It was particularly eerie the way those blue eyes were staring back at us, but the crisp dress shirt underneath the tailored suit gave the singer's frame a trim appearance. "I recall my mother listening to Patsy Cline. Hearing her songs still brings back memories of Mom dancing in the kitchen and singing into a spatula."

I'm joining Heidi up ahead. I'm a cat, not a fish. All these sappy tearjerkers are getting me wet down here.

"You mentioned that she was friends with my mother. I still find that amazing." It was also hard to picture Liam as a little boy. "I wonder if they ever kept in touch after Mom moved to New York City."

"I don't believe so," Liam replied, leaving behind Frank to stand in front of Tony. Who made these wax figures? Heidi and I had watched a movie years ago about a serial killer encasing their victims in wax. I shuddered in revulsion at the memory. Now that I knew what Ted was and that he was walking around with a heart of wax, I had mixed feelings. "From what I understand, your mother cut all ties with everyone she left behind in Paramour Bay."

"Mom has been known to hold a grudge or two." My statement got the reaction I was looking for, and I laughed along with Liam. "Seriously, she's still trying to get me to move back to the city after all this time."

"I hope that she doesn't succeed in that endeavor." I could feel the weight of Liam's warm gaze on me, and I was pretty sure that the temperature of the room had risen a few degrees. I didn't feel bad for the wax figures in the least. "I think the odds are in my favor, considering you just signed a three-year lease."

"So, you're saying there's another date in our immediate future? One that doesn't include the rest of the town's population?" I asked lightheartedly, following Liam through another doorway. For another brief moment, I'd forgotten all about Norman Palmer's wallet. A quick look over my shoulder didn't reveal any red silk material. "Maybe this time we can leave the townsfolk, our double date partners, and my overzealous mother behind. I guess we didn't think this through very well, did we?"

"I don't know about that." Liam was looking at the wax figure of Gary Cooper. I've never been good at history, specific years, or precise dates, but I was pretty sure he was an actor in the mid-to-late 1920s on into the 60s. Just so you know, I wasn't staring at the handsome movie star. "Midnight isn't too far away."

The promise of a lingering kiss to ring in the New Year caused a litany of goosebumps to cover my arms, and I'm relatively certain my cheeks were as red as the silk on Greta Garbo's lovely dress.

I turned my head so quickly that the nerve in my neck zinged. You know the one I'm talking about...the one that brings tears to your eyes. I rested my palm in the curve of my neck in hopes of easing the piercing neck pain.

Karma. She'll sneak up on you every time.

Leo.

He'd known this was the place where Norman Palmer lost his wallet all along.

I just checked. Nothing is underneath the red silk dress. You can enjoy the rest of the evening with Liam.

How was I going to search for Mr. Palmer's billfold without Liam asking me a ton of questions I couldn't answer?

"There you are!" Heidi exclaimed, coming out of another room to our left. She was like my personal genie, always coming up with answers and granting wishes. "Liam, there's an actual exhibit of 'The Andy Griffith Show' that you've just got to see in the next room. Can you believe that? Jack's looking at Barney Fife right now, but I need to borrow Raven for just a second, if you don't mind."

If I wasn't so against this, I'd be swooning over Heidi's ability to divide and conquer.

"Is something wrong?" Liam asked, not making a move toward the other room.

"Girl stuff," Heidi whispered, leaning in and making it appear that her problem could only be solved by her best friend. "I happen to know Raven has a safety pin in her purse for emergencies just like this. Give us one minute, tops."

Liam nodded in commiseration, not that he could ever

understand what it was like to wear women's clothing. Carrying around the equivalent of two cantaloupes all the time was physically draining without the proper equipment.

TMI, Raven. TMI.

Both Heidi and I watched Liam duck out of the room, though I doubt her gaze was as low as mine. The man really did have a nice—

"There you are," my mother's voice startled us from behind. I didn't do the best job of smothering my groan of frustration, which was evident by the way her eyebrows made the perfect V. "I travel all this way, and you throw me to the mercy of Cora Barnes, of all people? Where did I go wrong raising you, child?"

I ask myself that same question each and every day.

"You went wrong when you lied and denied me this part of my heritage," I whispered back honestly, looking over her shoulder to make sure the coast was clear. "And now we have a chance to finally clear Nan's name. I can't believe she didn't do that herself. Or you, especially when Cora and Beverly started to say mean things to you back in high school."

"There are some things that are better left buried, Raven."

They know about Ted.

"Oh, dear Lord."

My mother's disconcerting gaze landed directly on Heidi, who now appeared as if she were a viewer of a tennis match looking back and forth. Once she realized that someone else was in the conversation—Leo—she set both hands on her hips in exasperation.

"Is there something we can do about this?" Heidi asked, her left eyebrow arching higher than usual.

I had to give Heidi props. My mother was waiting for her to make a mistake and bring up witchcraft in a public setting.

Not for love nor money would I admit that Heidi and I *have* spoken about it, though very cautiously in fear of someone overhearing what was said.

"Something about..." My mother took it one step further, but Leo immediately cut her off.

Me, Leo piped up. *I'm thinking she's onto something. Could there be a spell so that a human can hear a familiar?*

"No," both Mom and I said in unison. It was bad enough that my mother heard everything Leo said, but Leo was mine to deal with.

I am, am I?

Well, technically he was my grandmother's familiar. I could summon one of my own, but then I'd have twice the problems and half the time to deal with each. With my luck, I'd probably get a songbird that I'd have to guard night and day from Leo. Regardless, I'd inherited him, and I didn't want another familiar to deal with.

I'm getting tingly all over. What do you think that means? Maybe my tail is about to go numb again.

"We are running out of time," I declared, ignoring Leo. He was making a bigger deal out of what I knew to be my own self-ishness. I couldn't deny that Leo was a pain in the buttocks, but he was also my lifeline to what Nan had known I needed. It was funny to think back to the first time I'd met him. I'd been ready to commit myself to a mental hospital. "I saw red silk fabric during the—"

"I get it," Regina asserted, holding up a hand to stop me from talking aloud about locater spells. It wasn't a surprise to see her manicured nails done to perfection. "Have you not been to the wax museum before, Raven? There are a ton of wax figures that have on red dresses or exhibits that have red silk tablecloths. It would be too noticeable for us to look underneath each and every one."

You know that I never like to agree with Regina, but she does have a point there.

"Not to mention that this place gets cleaned every week by a professional cleaning service," Heidi added to the conversation, not helping my plight. She twisted her full lips as she thought through our predicament. "We could split up. Did you notice anything else in your...uh, daydream?"

Daydream? Am I having a short-term memory lapse or is Heidi drunk?

I sighed at the fact that nothing was ever easy, and having my mother here didn't help matters in the least.

You won't get an argument from me on that one.

"It's your fault, anyway," I muttered, shaking my head when Heidi would have taken offense to my accusation. I clarified, already knowing how my mother was going to react. "It's Leo's fault. He was the one who dimed us out and brought her here."

And who exactly is to blame for that? You gave me no choice but to call in the cavalry.

"And Leo was right to do so." Regina looked over her shoulder upon hearing voices becoming louder. When the coast was still clear, she focused on me. I was amazed when she finally relented, though with a stipulation. I should have known it was too good to be true. "I'll help you find Norman Palmer's wallet if you promise to drop this pursuit of clearing our family name should there be nothing inside the billfold of any measurable significance."

Leo's deafening silence told me this was a trick. Did she know that there was nothing in the wallet that would point toward the murderer?

"Leo?" I called out cautiously, bracing myself for his response.

"Leave the cat out of this," Regina warned, her green eyes sparkling with determination. She tucked her small clutch underneath her arm. "Do we have a deal or not?"

Leo remained silent, all but forcing my hand.

"Fine," I relented, hoping there was a way out of this arrangement if I came out on the losing end. I wasn't a sore loser, but I also didn't appreciate being tricked—and by my own mother, no less. "What can you do that I haven't already tried? Leo's probably already told you that I attempted to revisit Norman Palmer's last few moments. All I saw was black. Well, it was a rippling blackness that I took for water. Could I be wrong?"

Quite often, as a matter of fact. As a rule, I pretty much dismiss all your guesswork as one hundred percent unreliable.

"Now you show up," I muttered as I took a quick look around the room. Just how long could Leo remain invisible? "Don't answer that."

I didn't want more worries added to my plate, and the way my mom pursed her red lips told me I *was* wrong about the blackness. What else could the flowing darkness be in the context of Mr. Palmer's murder?

"What is your mother doing?" Heidi whispered with a slightly induced wobble of panic in her voice. I was honestly too dumbfounded to answer, because Mom had closed her eyes and begun reciting an enchantment I'd never heard before. "Tell her to stop before someone comes in here."

I knew from experience that it was too late to prevent my mother from completing the spell. Truthfully, I didn't want to. She'd shielded me from this my entire childhood, even admitting to me upon my discovery of our ancestors that she'd long ago given up this life.

Now don't get me wrong.

Mom had come to my rescue once before with the use of magic, but I'd thought it was a common spell she'd learned from Nan when she was young. You know, something easy to remember. But this? It was a complicated incantation that not even coffee would have given me the stimulated brain cells to recall hours later.

I don't believe it.

"Raven, do something," Heidi called out, nudging my arm.

I was too focused on the slight modification of the air around us. It was like walking across the carpet during the winter months with cozy socks—electrical in nature.

It seems your mother never gave up practicing witchcraft. Will wonders never cease?

"Raven." Heidi was still attempting to garner my attention, but the vision of my mother using her gift was too fascinating for me to take my eyes off her. "We're about to have a major problem here."

It was then that I noticed movement over my mother's shoulder in the form of none other than Rye Dolgiram.

Fifteen

"RYE, it's good to see you again," Heidi exclaimed, quickly stepping around my mother and blocking his advance. "Were you finally able to get that casement fixed over at the inn? I know that Gertie was..."

"Mom," I whispered as I reached out to touch her arm. Heidi was busy keeping Rye occupied to give me time to warn my mother. I'd never had anyone interrupt me during an enchantment, so I wasn't sure what would happen if I jarred her back to reality. "Mom, you need to—"

The need to scare you now overwhelms me.

"You're not helping, Leo," I whispered, making sure that Rye couldn't see me as I stepped closer to my mom. "Mom, you need to—"

"I'm well aware we're not alone, dear." Regina lifted her lashes and stared at me as if nothing had happened. "You'll find what you're looking for in the Ice Cream Shop exhibit."

I'm feeling a bit...sentimental. Regina hasn't lost her touch.

A group of people entered the room, seemingly having the same purpose as Rye in touring the other rooms of the wax museum. At least, I think that's why Rye left the party. Had he come to the party alone?

Stay clear of him, Raven.

"Who is that?" my mother asked warily, turning on her heels to see who Heidi had purposefully delayed with her charm. Mom looked Rye over from head to toe, coming to the same agreement as Leo. "Stay away from that one."

"Don't you think for a moment this gets you off the hook," I cautioned her, taking hold of her arm. "You said you left this world behind."

"I did."

You have a funny way of demonstrating that fact, Regina.

"You stood right in front of me and cast a spell to find a lost object," I reminded her in a harsh tone, knowing we were running out of time. Rye's dark gaze had landed on me and my mother. "You didn't leave anything behind. You hid your abilities, and then lied about it to me."

"Raven, we will not be discussing this here." My mother had a tendency not to only get the last word in on an argument, but to also shut one down at her convenience. "You made a deal with me, and I expect you to follow through."

She's got you there.

"It's not a valid agreement if you already know what's in the wallet," I warned, having no intention of bringing my investigation to a halt. "And I have to wonder, Mom. How do you know what's in Norman Palmer's wallet when you weren't even born yet?"

Um, she's a witch? Raven, are you sure it's only me with short-term memory loss or is it spreading like a cold?

"Go retrieve the wallet and then we'll talk." Regina studied Rye a little bit longer than warranted, most likely gauging his character. He had a dangerous quality about him, but I couldn't put my finger on why. "I'll rejoin the party and try to delay anyone wanting to take a tour. It's going on eleven o'clock, so I'm sure everyone will be focused on the ball strung up from the ceiling. Remember, a deal is a deal."

Mom had baited me into a trap, but I would do what was needed to find a way around the ruse she'd conjured in regard to the wallet deal.

My whiskers are already twitching.

Leo's bent whiskers tended to tic when something wasn't right, similar to when my palm became heated with the energy I derived from the earth. Rye had switched his gaze from my mother, who'd walked past him with her head held high, to me.

It's him. I don't like that man.

Leo had made such a claim before, but there was nothing we could do about his dislike of the handyman right now. I needed to find Mr. Palmer's wallet so that Liam and I could then be together when the clock struck midnight.

"Well, it was nice talking to you again." Heidi wiggled her fingers and then made a point to look in my direction. "Are you ready to rejoin Jack and Liam?"

The lesser of two evils. I can dig it.

"Yes, we should join our dates," I replied, nodding toward Rye so that he wouldn't think I was being rude. "They were near the Andy Griffith exhibit, I believe."

Had Rye really come alone? It wasn't that I hadn't attended functions alone before. I used to go to a Sunday afternoon movie nearly every weekend when none of my friends were available. There was nothing wrong with being happy with oneself, and Rye certainly struck me as a loner. Still, it was rather odd to come to something like this without a date.

I'm here without a date, thanks to Detective Jack Swanson. You want to take a swing at me, too?

"You aren't even supposed to be here," I murmured, falling into step beside Heidi as we made our way out of the 1920s exhibit. "And you know something about that wallet that my mother doesn't or else you would have helped me find it before now."

I plead the fifth, sixth, and all the rest of them.

"Wait a second," I exclaimed, halting our progress. The Andy Griffith exhibit was in sight, as well as Liam and Jack. They were in deep conversation and hadn't caught sight of us. "Heidi, my mother didn't perform an incantation."

She didn't?

"What do you mean?" Heidi asked in confusion. "We saw her do it."

"No, we didn't," I corrected, recognizing the difference between static electricity and the energy it takes to initiate a spell. She'd tried to throw me off, and she'd almost succeeded. "Mom knew exactly where Norman Palmer's wallet was this entire time. She made me accept her deal, fake a casting, and told me where to find the billfold all to keep me from finding out the truth."

She did? Ohhhh, now it's coming back to me.

"Leo, that is not short-term memory loss," I snapped, a part of me wishing I'd chosen a different time to dive into this old murder. Liam and Jack were now looking our way, so I was running out of time to explain. "Mom must have used her gift to do the exact thing I did back when she was in high school."

Hey, you're pretty good at filling in the missing pieces once you get started.

"So why doesn't your mother just come clean?" Heidi asked, pasting a smile on her face as we started to walk toward our dates. "Unless Regina found out something horrible she doesn't want you to know."

"Did you get everything sorted out?" Jack asked as we got closer, although he'd prevented me from answering Heidi's question.

You might say we sorted things out.

"Yes, much better," Heidi replied, gesturing toward the display. "Hey, those wax figures aren't too bad. Barney looks exactly like the real Barney."

"I personally think the Mayberry jail cell is a nice touch," Liam said, pointing at the cot inside the small cell. I couldn't help but wonder if Nan had belonged in some secure place like that. Had Mom discovered that Nan was the one who actually murdered Mr. Palmer? Had she driven all the way to Paramour Bay from the city to stop me from finding out that my grandmother was a cold-blooded killer? "I'm pretty sure Rita Carter designed the exhibit this way to mimic our cell. It's a pretty good likeness. Then again, maybe Sheriff Tripol renovated the station to mimic Mayberry's."

"You have a jail cell at the station?" I'd never seen anything of the sort. "Where?"

"Yes, we do have a place to hold the occasional intoxicated individual or shoplifter," Liam replied with a big smile. "And it's through the door next to the restroom."

"I thought that was a supply closet."

Although now that I imagined the police station in my mind, there was a window in between the two doors. It must have been installed there to keep an eye on the prisoner.

So much for your investigative skills.

"I like the fishing poles," Jack commented, mimicking the sport. Was it a sport? I'm sure Otis would agree. "Liam, we'll have to go fishing in the spring."

We slowly began walking once again, taking in the various television exhibits from the 1960s. This place was so full of history that I couldn't understand having something so grand hidden away in such a small town. Then again, Paramour Bay needed to be known for something, I guess.

And it shouldn't be witchcraft.

It was easy to ignore Leo this time, because something had brushed my hand. At first, I thought I'd veered into Liam's path and was about to apologize. It was in that exact moment that I realized he'd initiated contact first. His warm fingers wrapped around mine as we continued to walk and take in the sights.

God, I need a puff or two of catnip to get me through this night.

I enjoyed my time with Liam as we continued through the many creative exhibits Rita Carter had put together. Alison had done a great job of keeping up with the times. I'd noted several recent actors and actresses, along with today's top-charting singers. Eventually, we reached the end of the building with no Ice Cream Parlor exhibit in sight.

I had a very important decision to make.

Choose wisely, grasshopper.

Did I ask discreetly about the non-exhibit or did I leave my quest for the truth behind while enjoying the rest of the evening? I figured we'd taken at least thirty minutes to make our way through the museum, if not longer.

Midnight couldn't be far away.

I should be home with Ted. Can we reconvene this so-called search for justice at another time?

It didn't escape me that both my mother and Leo had both gotten what they'd wanted this New Year's Eve, while I still hadn't come even close to clearing Nan's name.

What I wanted was to be home with a pipeful of my catnip to ring in the New Year.

"We should probably invite your mother to join our table," Liam suggested to me as we leisurely began our way back through the various rooms. Heidi kept looking over her shoulder, but she was very careful with her facial expressions in case Liam caught her in the act. "Unless she and Cora suddenly made amends."

Who knew the sheriff had a sense of humor? He's a funny guy.

"Nothing is out of the realm of possibility," I said with a laugh, figuring the odds of Mom and Cora letting bygones be bygones had as much chance as Leo giving up catnip.

That sounds statistically about right—zero.

"Oh, there you are," Alison said with relief, coming from absolutely nowhere. Seriously, she hadn't been walking toward us from the direction we came. Instead, she'd materialized from somewhere behind Charlie Chaplin. "Liam, it seems that in all the commotion with the cake falling onto Cora that her purse has gone missing. She's asking for you to look into it."

Looks like Liam has to work. Oh, well. Let's head back the way we came, shall we?

"I think you might have been right about this party not being the best choice for our first date," Liam murmured, releasing my hand and stepping forward to do his job. I already missed the warmth of his fingers. "It's no problem, Alison. I'll take care of it."

"I'll help so we can get this over with quickly," Jack offered.

"Follow me through the storage area." Alison looked beautiful in a cream sweater dress accented with gold ribbon throughout the fabric. She gave us a wink before she turned to face Charlie Chaplin. "Don't mind the clutter. This is where we store the wax figures we only put on display at certain times of the year."

Raven, why don't we let them take the shortcut? Didn't you want to see if we missed the Ice Cream Parlor exhibit? We should walk back through in case we accidentally bypassed it.

Heidi and I shared a knowing look, both of us believing we'd find what we were looking for behind good ol' Charlie. Liam and Jack followed closely behind Alison, allowing Heidi and me to walk a little bit slower. I wasn't too surprised to find a hidden door behind the exhibit, but the sudden energy that filled my palm had certainly caught me off guard.

Ignore it. I'm sure the sensation was left over from Liam's lingering touch. You said it yourself, there's an underlying chemistry between the two of you. Let's get going. Keep up.

I ignored Leo's attempt at getting me to hurry along without obtaining a good look at the chamber we were passing through. There was no other way to describe the room. It was rather dark with the exception of an overhead hanging bare lightbulb.

Shadows were being cast by numerous wax figures, some covered in sheets while others were visible to the naked eye. A layer of dust covered their shoulders. Noticeable cobwebs that glistened in the golden light had me wondering just how many spiders were living in this room.

Spiders? That's not good. I'm not exactly a fan of them, Raven.

I couldn't worry about spiders when all I could think about—besides Norman Palmer's wallet—was Fred.

"Alison, did a man named Fred ever work here? Maybe for your mother, back in the day?"

"What an odd question," Alison said before reaching for the doorknob on another door. "I don't believe so. I've never heard the name before."

Ask her about spiders. Are they those little ones or the big massive guys that eat cats whole? Hairy or just scary? Inquiring cats need to know.

Liam looked over his shoulder as if he wanted to ask me why I'd asked about a stranger, but Alison was trying to usher them through the door.

"Raven, look," Heidi whispered, grabbing my forearm to stop me from getting too close to the exit that Alison was currently guiding Jack and Liam through. "There's another door, but it doesn't lead out to the main area."

Mice are one thing. Spiders are something completely different that obviously shouldn't be allowed to roam free to prey on domesticated animals. Can we go, please?

"Raven? Heidi?" Alison called out to us, having remained at the door while looking back at us with concern. "Is everything alright?"

Heidi always had luck on her side. Seriously, she'd be the cartoon character always one step ahead of disaster. A piano pushed out the window? She'd have already walked past the spot where it landed. An icicle falling from above? She'd be two steps ahead of where it crashed into a million pieces.

Now?

She whipped a cell phone from out of nowhere and held it up with a smile.

"Marilyn Monroe is standing right here! I have to get my picture taken," Heidi gushed, shoving her phone into my hand. I'd already had my clutch in between my elbow and hip, so I was able to grab the cell and play along. "You don't mind, do you, Alison?"

Oh, our Heidi is a quick one, isn't she?

That she was, but I wasn't so sure Alison was going to allow us to stay behind on our own. The woman's hesitation was clearly obvious, but Cora's dramatic flair could be heard over the music drifting into the storage area.

"One picture," Alison cautioned, her eyes scanning the chamber for what could obviously turn into an insurance claim. Boxes were also scattered in and around the wax figures, most likely containing items for specific exhibits. "I'll leave the door cracked, but please make sure you close it behind you when you're done. We don't allow guests to be in this part of the building, and I don't want someone using this entrance to exit the main lounge."

And just like that, Alison disappeared from view as she carefully allowed the door to stay open an inch. In a blink of an eye, Leo materialized with one front paw and one back paw in the air. His green eyes widened as he became alert to everything around us.

Did that wax figure just move?

"Stop it," I admonished, my anxiety level already dialed on high. The last thing I needed to deal with was a scaredy cat. "Heidi, this is a bad idea."

That's the first smart thing you've said this evening.

"I thought you wanted to find Norman Palmer's wallet?" Heidi began to carefully tiptoe her way through the various wax figures after she'd snagged her cell phone from my hand—which, by the way, was still warm. And since when had Heidi developed the type of courage to pick her way through life-sized figurines? "What if there's some hidden exhibit behind that door? We'll just take a quick peek, and then we'll rejoin the party."

I was worried about you putting us in danger. I underestimated her, didn't I? And let's not forget those spiders. Do you see any?

Heidi activated the flashlight on her phone, but I couldn't

allow her to do this on her own. I didn't do well with guilt, which was proven by the fact that Heidi was here with me and knew all my life's secrets.

You just had to tell her you were a witch. This all started with your loud mouth.

Heidi had finally made it to the door that was behind numerous wax figures, but she stopped just shy of reaching for the door handle. Her curls bounced when she started to wave me forward, wanting me to see whatever it was she'd found.

"Jackpot," Heidi squealed, leaning down on her black high heels. I followed suit until both of us were kneeling in front of red silk. "Quick. I'll hold the flashlight on my phone steady while you lift the fabric."

And there was my Heidi.

She's one smart lady. Listen, before you search underneath that material, give me a second to get to higher ground in case a spider comes scurrying out.

Leo shuddered and then tentatively jumped on a box that would give him some leverage and space from whatever we might find. You won't believe the label on the box, either—*Ice Cream Parlor Exhibit.*

Had my mother used a spell to locate the wallet? Or had she known all along the whereabouts of the billfold...because she'd been in this exact same spot so many years ago?

I remember now, though this storage room didn't have this many cobwebs back then. I'm beginning to think that Alison's weekly cleaning crew are a bit lax with their dusting duties.

I caught the red silk in between my thumb and index finger, pulling it to the side very tentatively. What if there *were* spiders underneath it?

"Is that..." Heidi's voice trailed off as we set our eyes on a black leather billfold. "Oh, wow."

Oh, wow was right. Not only had we found Norman Palmer's wallet, but we'd also discovered a black-knit ski mask that could only have been his. He must have used it to break into the museum, wanting to hide his identity.

You're actually piecing this all together rather well, you know.

"This witchcraft thing is so freaking cool," Heidi whispered, moving the phone a bit to focus on the wallet. "Go ahead. Pick it up. What's inside of it?"

Considering my mother had sent me on this wild goose chase, most likely nothing.

You would be correct.

Imagine my surprise when a picture fell out after I'd opened the wallet.

That can't be right.

Before I could reach for the photograph, an undeniable downright eerie creaking noise filled the air.

What. Was. That?

I held my breath as both Heidi and I turned around to the door that was no longer cloaked in darkness. Heidi had shifted the light on her phone toward the door just in time for the wooden exit to slowly open.

Run for your lives!

Sixteen

HIDE!

I didn't have to relay the directives Leo was yelling randomly, because Heidi smothered a scream as she quickly fumbled with her phone to turn off the flashlight feature. Her attempt didn't matter, because the overhead lightbulb provided enough light that we couldn't hide in the shadows anyway.

I did the only thing I could and yanked the red fabric until it covered both of us.

That was smart.

I couldn't bring myself to remind Leo that he could have easily made himself invisible. He sometimes forgot his gift during times of high anxiety. This easily counted as one of those harrowing moments.

Don't. Say. A. Word.

Heidi and I grabbed each other's hands as we sat huddled together in hiding—with Leo squished between us—hoping that whoever had entered through the secret door didn't notice anything different about the room.

How could they?

This storage area was a jumbled mess, littered with boxes and wax figurines behind the scenes.

The faintest sound of someone taking a step toward us had me squeezing Heidi's fingers tighter than before. Leo must have put one of his front paws on my leg, because his claws sank into my flesh deep enough to bring tears to my eyes. There was nothing I could do but hold my breath, listening for any other sound that would let me know we'd all been made.

"...neither Heidi nor Raven came out that I noticed." Alison's voice became clear as she obviously came back into the room looking for us. "Maybe they decided to go back through the museum to take more pictures."

I'd expected there to be a shuffle of footsteps from the intruder retreating the way he or she had come from, but there was only silence. Had I missed the scuffling sounds when Alison had opened the other door?

For the record, I didn't hear anything, either.

"Do you mind if I go through the room to the other side?" Liam asked, the concern in his tone easily distinguishable. Guilt flooded my system that I was currently hiding from him underneath this silk cloth, but what could Heidi and I do now? "I'll be able to catch up with them sooner than if I go around the building from the foyer."

You should feel guilty. We shouldn't even be here in the first place. This is all your fault, and I'm not to blame for what will happen if I feel a spider start burrowing in my fur.

"Of course," Alison agreed. Seconds later, we heard the sound of Liam crossing the filthy floor. Leo wasn't the only one who was afraid a spider might crawl on him. I was still in a kneeling position, but what was to say a spider wouldn't crawl up my boot and onto my knee? "I'll just go ahead and turn the light off after you've gone out the other door."

She wouldn't dare.

I wasn't sure why Alison shutting off the light would be a problem for Leo. Couldn't cats see in the dark?

I can? Who sold you that load of tripe?

Leo definitely didn't have short-term memory loss. Whatever black magic Nan had used obviously affected short and long-term memory equally.

Well, I certainly remember why we're hiding underneath a red silk tablecloth. You couldn't leave well enough alone, and now the truth is going to come out.

The faintest echo of a latch catching meant Liam had closed the door to the other side of the museum. Shortly after, Alison switched off the light and shut us inside.

Why look at that. I can *see in the dark. Will miracles never cease?*

All three of us remained still, which told me that I wasn't the only one who thought we weren't alone in here. I released Heidi's hand until I was able to rest my hand on Leo. After all, he was the one who could see in the dark.

You'd use me as bait? Do you think so little of me? No, don't answer that.

Leo was the only one who could see if someone was still in the room with us. If Heidi and I couldn't see in the darkness, then neither could the intruder.

Well, when you put it like that...

Leo ever so slowly began to leave the safety of the red silk tablecloth. Pretty soon, his soft tail disappeared from my fingers.

Heidi was tapping me on the knee, most likely wondering what the plan was. I could only wait for Leo to report back, so I once again took ahold of Heidi's hand. Together, we remained as completely still as the wax figures around us.

I don't see anything. Nada. Zilch.

I fumbled around until Heidi understood that I wanted her to turn on the flashlight on her phone. The moment I could sense that she was about to press the button, I snatched the red silk and whipped it from our heads.

The bright light landed right on Leo, whose back was arched with a tail as bushy as Mayor Sander's eyebrows.

"Are we seriously locked in here?"

Heidi didn't even pretend to have composure. Neither did I, for that matter. The door that had begun to slowly open earlier was now closed. Still, something wasn't right and my hand was practically catching on fire.

I could be at home with my pipe. Instead, I'm—ack! Spiders!

Leo was there one minute and gone the next with what was a strangled meow.

"I don't think the doors lock," I murmured, reaching out and directing her phone to the floor. I'd somehow lost my purse when I'd picked up Norman Palmer's billfold, as well as the photograph that had fallen to the ground. "Alison didn't use a key when she brought us through here, so I think the door is just concealed from one side and easily opened from our side. Let's find that picture and then get out of here. Something isn't right."

"Tell me about it," Heidi said practically incoherently, directing the light to the closed door. "Raven, I didn't hear anyone leave."

"Neither did I, but everything looks the same." By this time, I'd picked up my purse. I unzipped the small clutch and pulled out my phone. It wasn't hard to find. There was only so much that could fit in a five-by-eight-sized square. "See?"

I'd pulled the flashlight up on my phone and was currently dragging the white beam slowly across the room. Heidi kept her sights on the door as I continued to scan the storage area.

There was no suppressing my shudder of aversion to the cobwebs glistening in the light. I tried to tell myself that it didn't matter, as long as the wax figures remained where they were and the boxes didn't suddenly pop open to reveal a killer clown.

Yes, I'm deathly afraid of clowns. That's never come up before now, but I thought I'd throw that tidbit out there, given the circumstances. You know, just in case one sprang up from one of the boxes and all you're left with is my silhouette through the wall.

I guess I could compare my fear to Leo's arachnophobia.

"Then let's get out of here," Heidi replied, though her response was hard to hear and kind of wobbly. "Did you grab the picture?"

"No." I redirected my phone so that I could locate the picture. It had been moved by the red silk when I'd thrown the tablecloth over our heads, but it didn't take me long to locate it. "Here it is. Now let's get out of here and figure out how we're going to make it seem like we were in the crowd the entire—"

What was I staring at?

Fred.

I'm pretty sure that my boots came off the floor at the sound of Leo's voice. He'd returned, though this time he was sitting on a box behind me. I'd startled Heidi to the point where she'd spun around in a circle, shining the light on anything that could have been responsible for my scare.

That photograph wasn't supposed to be in there. I wonder if Ms. Drake put it back when she and your mother were here many years ago. That would explain why your mother thought it was safe for you to find the billfold.

"It's just Leo," I told her after I'd gotten my heart rate under control. My mother had made a mistake. That rarely happened, but I would take what I could get. This meant I could still look into clearing Nan's name. "Heidi, look at this."

I so don't want to be here when your mother finds out. Oh, this isn't good.

"Is the picture of someone we know?" Heidi asked, scooting closer to me so we could see who was in the picture together. Only when I'd picked up the photograph, the back of it had been facing me. There was a name displayed in masculine handwriting in black ink. "Fred. Turn it over! Maybe we can show this around to Otis, Alison, Albert, and the rest of the people who'd been involved in the case."

Oh, I don't think I'd do that if I were you.

I didn't waste time flipping over the picture, all but ignoring Leo's warning. We were running out of time, and the answer I'd sought for days was in my hands.

"Whaaatttt?" Heidi asked, carrying out the question longer than necessary. "That's just...whaaatttt?"

Honestly, I was just as shocked as she was.

The man staring back at us in the black and white photograph was none other than Fred Astaire.

Fred.

"Leo, this is Fred Astaire."

Seventeen

YES, *Fred.*

"I'm pretty sure Fred Astaire didn't die until the 1980s," Heidi whispered, giving me a shrug when I cast a questioning glance her way. "What can I say? I'm a huge fan of *Funny Face.* Is that *Fred* Fred or a Fred like Ted?"

"Leo, was the real Fred Astaire ever in Paramour Bay?"

Ohhhhh, I knew there was a reason you weren't supposed to find out about Fred.

"What does that mean?"

Before Leo could answer my question, one of the wax figures moved.

Literally.

It. Moved.

I don't have to tell you that wax figures shouldn't move. Well, if you discount Ted. But he was an anomaly. Unless Nan had made more of him? Wow. That was too much to take in, and Heidi didn't even have time to scream as my arm seemed to have a will of its own.

Somewhere inside of me was an inherent need to protect

us, and nothing I did could stop the current from traveling the length of my arm.

No, no, no! Don't—

Within a millisecond, my hand released an energy ball that was ten times brighter than the light from our tiny flashlights. It hit the wax figure with enough force to send it back six feet into a stack of boxes. That was enough time for Heidi and me to scramble out from the other wax figures and collection of boxes we'd been hiding behind and run toward the door.

It should have been a clean getaway.

Should have *being the operative words.*

It would have been had my boot not gotten caught in the red silk fabric.

Down I went in an ungraceful faceplant, all the while Heidi holding onto my arm. I had to give my best friend credit —she hadn't left me behind. With that said, now wasn't the most opportune time for my accident-prone tendencies to come forth.

"Raven?"

I had to be hearing things.

The individual calling out my name sounded like—

My mental break didn't stop me from struggling to my knees and eventually my feet. Heidi never once stopped her attempt to pull me up off the filthy floor.

"It's me."

It couldn't be.

It is, and how could you do that to Ted?

"Ted?"

Yes, Ted. He might irritate me more than a little, but even he doesn't deserve to be melted and thrown six feet onto the floor. Did you see that spectacle before you faceplanted? That was quite impressive.

"Leo," I warned, brushing off the cobwebs. I was tempted to wipe them on his fur to attract the eight-legged creatures, but even I wasn't that mean. Just as I hadn't meant to hurt Ted, but he wasn't even supposed to be here! "Don't push me."

I see you have a vindictive side. Good to know.

I swear I could hear Leo's shudder.

Duly noted.

"I didn't mean to…" I let my words trail off, because there was no excuse for me practically incinerating Ted—who was technically a stolen wax figure. Oh, my. Could he have melted completely? "Ted, I'm so sorry!"

You should be. You almost blew him to smithereens.

"Ted, what on earth are you doing here?" Heidi exclaimed, shining her phone in the direction of the carnage left behind by the energy source that I had hurled from the palm of my hand. "Was that you coming through the door?"

"Yes."

We both managed to reach Ted without another incident. Heidi grabbed him under his left arm while I did the same to his right, all the while maintaining our hold on our phones. It was a miracle that no one had heard our screams or Ted all but being hurled through the air. The crushed boxes and whatever might have been in them were most likely unsalvageable.

Then again, it was really close to midnight. I'm sure the music was loud and the partygoers were ready to ring in the New Year. Any sounds we made in this room were probably stifled.

"How did you get here?" I attempted to wipe away the dust and cobwebs that were sticking to the fabric of Ted's suit, but it was a useless endeavor. "And where does that door lead to?"

"In from the parking lot."

"Ted." Heidi shoved her purse my way, stepping directly in front of Ted so that she could hold onto both his arms. Thankfully, he appeared unharmed. Maybe golems weren't that easy to harm. "Look at me."

The two of them made quite the pair—a gentle giant and a petite-sized blonde. Ted didn't seem to have any concept of time, but Heidi was well aware that our absences were probably being noticed. Liam and Jack would not hesitate to initiate some type of search party for us.

"Why are you here, Ted?" Heidi didn't waste time, and she got right to the point. "Why are you back at the wax museum?"

"To stop Raven from discovering the truth."

"What truth, Ted?" What could be so bad that everyone thought it was better to keep me in the dark than to shed light on the past? "What don't you want me to know?"

"That I'm like Fred."

I promptly looked down at the photograph in my hand, and suddenly everything in the crime reports made sense. Well, not everything, but enough that I could make some connections.

"Fred was like you," I whispered upon discovery. "That's why there was no mention of Fred in the reports, because he didn't actually exist."

"I don't want to be the old me."

It took me a few seconds to figure out what he meant. My heart ached upon comprehending his true meaning—he didn't want to go back to being an inanimate wax object. Heidi had already wrapped her arms around Ted's waist and pressed her cheek against his chest in reassurance. It was clear that he wasn't sure how to respond to her empathy, but he did manage to pat her awkwardly on the back of her head.

"Do something," Heidi instructed rather harshly in her

attempt to reassure Ted that he wouldn't end up like Fred...not that I know what actually happened to the other wax figure.

I waited for Leo to make a crack about Ted's discomfort or my lack of knowledge of the situation, but it never came. As a matter of fact, Leo hadn't said anything in quite some time.

"Ted, I can promise you that I would never take away..." I was unsure how to phrase my oath, but I put it in context of what I would want to hear. "I would never take away your humanity."

My mother's warning to Heidi this past weekend on the phone that witchcraft came with a lot of responsibility took on a whole new meaning.

Nan had given life to an inanimate object. Now *that* came with responsibilities.

Had my mother figured out what my grandmother had done? Was that the reason she left town?

Ted could now see, smell, hear, taste, and touch. He was also frightened to lose what he'd been given, which meant he'd learned to feel emotions just like a real man.

"Ted, did Nan stop Norman Palmer because he'd discovered what she'd done to bring Fred to life?" It was all becoming rather clear, and I didn't like the puzzle I'd put together. I didn't even wait for Ted to answer me. I gave a rundown of the timeline I thought occurred. "Norman broke into the wax museum to confirm his suspicions. It's why he needed a crowbar and that black ski mask. He then lost his wallet while rummaging around in the storage areas. Norman had no choice but to insert himself into Nan's life to get close to her in search of more answers, and he somehow found out the truth —that Nan had used magic to bring the wax figure of Fred Astaire to life."

"Not to nitpick, but the real Fred Astaire *was* in fact alive at the time," Heidi interjected with a bit of Hollywood history, holding up a hand when I shot her a daggered look. "Look, we've got to get back to the party. Jack and Liam have probably sent out a countywide BOLO for us by now. We need to somehow rejoin the guests without anyone realizing we've been gone this long. Where is Leo? Did he—"

Heidi and I jumped when the door that Liam had gone through suddenly opened, revealing my mother—who was not in the best of moods from what I could gather.

And whose fault is that, little Miss Detective?

My mother wasn't alone. Leo had purposefully sought her out.

What was I supposed to do? Let you find out that Fred murdered Norman?

"...do you mean Raven found out? How? And what are they doing in..."

Light poured in from the Charlie Chaplin exhibit as my mother stood in the doorway, staring at us in horror.

That was my reaction, too. I was blindsided.

Well, it was mine, too. I couldn't have heard Leo say that Fred was the one to kill Norman.

Could I?

Maybe. Did I let that slip?

"Leo," Regina muttered in disbelief before hastily closing the door behind her. "What on earth is going on here?"

This is what I've been trying to tell you. While you've been out there partying, your daughter is about to experience the same revelation you did in high school.

"I'm just as lost as everyone else," Heidi muttered, unable to hear Leo's confessions. She pressed her fingers to her forehead. "I want to point out once again that we're running out of time."

Raven, they are not confessions. I have nothing to confess to. Well, unless you count the time that I broke the lamp in the bedroom. It was in the way of my tail. There was nothing I could do.

"Is it true?" I asked my mother, ignoring Leo completely in my quest for answers. My chest tightened to the point of pain. "Did a reanimated wax figure of Fred Astaire kill Norman Palmer?"

I don't need to point out how ridiculous that sounds, now do I?

Heidi didn't have to be told that I wasn't going anywhere until I had answers. No one would come looking for us in here, because Alison and Liam had already come through the storage room. I still had time to learn the truth about Nan, no matter how heartbreaking the reveal might be.

"Let me get the light," Heidi said softly, touching my shoulder reassuringly as she made her way over to the door that led to the main area. She reached up and pulled the string so that the single light bulb gave all of us the ability to see without using the flashlights on our phones.

I could see, but that's beside the point, isn't it?

Both my mother and I took a step toward Leo, who was perched on one of the boxes Ted had crushed with his right arm trying to break his fall.

Okay. I'll be quiet now.

"In a manner of speaking," my mother reluctantly admitted, clearly not wanting to have this discussion. She waved a hand in the air in helplessness, but I didn't relent. "It was in self-defense, you see. Norman wasn't a businessman looking at the shops here in town the way Otis had originally suspected. Norman was a journalist who'd heard that Fred Astaire had been spotted in Paramour Bay. Unfortunately, Norman quickly suspected that all was not right, and he began investigating the museum."

Something wasn't adding up, but I was too stunned at the realization that Nan had covered up a murder committed by her creation. What kind of person did that? Leo was always stressing that our gift of witchcraft not be used for selfish purposes, but that's exactly what Nan had done in this case.

"Nan covered up for Fred?" I asked, unable to keep my incredulity hidden. "Nan allowed something she created to take a life?"

May I speak?

"No," both my mother and I said in unison.

"Raven." My mother stepped forward, almost as if she wanted to draw me in for a hug, but I couldn't take her offer of comfort. I stepped back, standing next to Heidi. "It's not what you—"

"You left town because Nan was just as guilty as her Fred Astaire golem."

Could we just call him Fred? He wasn't actually *Mr. Astaire.*

"That's not quite the reason," Regina said somewhat reluctantly, her knuckles turning white as she tightened her grip on her purse. "But seeing what happens when we pull out all the stops to protect our family secret did have something to do with it."

Just tell her. All of these secrets are giving me a headache.

"You abandoned her." Ted was frowning at my mother. A blond lock of his hair was hanging down his forehead, causing him to look like a little boy. It was clear that he was hurt on Nan's behalf and needed to defend her. "Miss Rosemary did the best she could."

Wellll, she could have done a better job on me...but nobody's perfect.

"My mother's best wasn't good enough," Regina exclaimed somewhat defensively. "Raven, now isn't the time or place to discuss this. Liam has been looking for you, and I'm sure by now he's organizing a search party. We should—"

"I know Liam is looking for me, but Heidi and I haven't been gone for more than twenty minutes." The time span might have felt like hours, but it wasn't. And I wasn't leaving this room until I got the answers I'd come here to find. "Out with it, Mom. No more lies. Nan created Fred. Norman figured out that Fred wasn't the real Fred, and then what? Fred killed Norman to keep him silent?"

Hmmm. I might have had that itty-bitty detail turned around.

"As I said, it wasn't quite like that." Regina straightened her shoulders and blurted out the opposite of my conclusion. "You see, Norman killed Fred. It wasn't the other way around."

Now that's a mic drop moment.

Eighteen

"WELL, we certainly didn't predict this outcome," Heidi muttered with a shake of her head. "I have to say...my family antics are quite boring compared to yours."

"Then who killed Norman?" I asked, in total agreement with Heidi that this was not the outcome I'd seen coming. "Did Nan kill Norman Palmer? Is that why you left town?"

Rosemary is probably spinning in her grave that you would think she was capable of such a horrible thing.

"It's not like anyone has corrected my assumptions, Leo." My patience had run its course. "If Nan didn't kill Norman Palmer and Fred didn't kill Norman Palmer...then who did?"

Get ready for a whopper.

"No one murdered Norman Palmer," Regina stated rather matter-of-factly, as if I should have known this all along. "Norman killed Fred before he fell into the lake off one of the piers after having attacked your grandmother's creation. The man couldn't swim. He simply drowned. It was a tragic accident, and one your grandmother had a very hard time accepting.

Golems are not easy to kill, mind you, but Norman had shoved Fred onto an iron pole that was sticking up between the boards. It must have pierced the exact spot where your grandmother had enclosed Fred's *shem*, which was the material component of the spell that gave him life. We never had another Fred after that."

We did, but you just didn't know about it until you met the new Fred—Ted.

No amount of witchcraft had prepared me for this, and no enchantments had aided in these discoveries. It was a quick lesson to learn that I was still an average woman with quite a bit of family issues.

A whole lot *of family issues, but who's counting?*

"Why not just tell me this from the beginning?" I asked, really confused as to why my mother hadn't come clean the moment I'd brought up Fred on the telephone. "Your behavior led me to believe that Nan might be a murderer."

That's true, Regina.

"You, too," I scolded Leo. "It was mean of both of you."

"Agreed," Heidi said softly, staring at Leo in disappointment.

I have short-term memory loss! Okay, there seems to be problems with my memory in general, but that was your grandmother's doing.

Bottom line?

There was technically no murder, meaning the town of Paramour Bay had a spotless record when it came to closing cases. Liam could never know that, because I would have to reveal my family secret.

You're learning, Raven. You're learning.

My mother surprised me when she tucked her purse underneath her elbow before closing the distance between us. She gently took my hands and tilted her head as she explained her stance.

"Your grandmother and I might not have seen things eye to eye, but she loved both of us very much. When you mentioned you were looking into Norman Palmer's death, I was afraid you would come to the same conclusion as I had back when I was in high school."

My mother looked down at our linked hands, a despondency coming over her that tugged at my heart.

Mine, too. See? She didn't give up the craft. That's the only explanation as to why I'm experiencing sympathy.

"Leo, I'm trying to speak with my daughter," Regina said rather sharply, giving both Leo and Ted a look that basically dared either one to speak. Both were smart and remained quiet. She then focused all of her attention on me. "Raven, I gave your grandmother a run for her money for years after believing I'd found out the truth about Norman Palmer's death. It all came to a head years later when I was pregnant with you, and by the time she finished explaining the true details of what happened...well, I realized that I couldn't bring you up in a world where someone would think nothing of murder."

"But—" I attempted to interrupt, but my mother didn't give me a chance.

"You see, Norman Palmer couldn't prove that anything was amiss and your grandmother was very good at covering her tracks. In the end, Norman believed that Fred—wax figure Fred—was attempting to impersonate the real Fred. They got into an altercation until one thing led to another and..."

Fred was dead.

"So, Norman never knew that Fred was a wax figure?"

"No, not to my knowledge." My mother squeezed my fingers until I was looking directly at her and not Leo or Ted.

"I do not regret giving you a childhood free of the responsibility of having so much power. I don't believe there was a right or wrong in that situation, but I couldn't allow you to believe your grandmother was a murderer. It was the reason I didn't want to talk about everything that happened all those years ago, but in your true stubborn fashion, you couldn't leave well enough alone. Trust me, it occurred to me to let you believe it in order to have you come home. But even I couldn't do that to my daughter, and I could sense Leo's worry all the way in New York City. I figured I had no choice but to come here and see to it myself that you didn't do anything foolish."

It is *becoming a regular habit of yours.*

"What about the rippling darkness that Raven saw when she attempted to recall Norman Palmer's last memories?" Heidi asked, taking the step that separated her from Ted. She rested a hand on his arm, reassuring him that we wouldn't allow any harm to come to him. "What was that about?"

"I had the same thing happen to me," Regina admitted, giving my hands one last squeeze before she released them. "I can only assume that Norman Palmer wasn't a nice man. I believe we saw into his soul and not through his eyes."

"That's downright creepy," Heidi murmured, wrapping her arms around herself in an attempt to ward off a shiver. I didn't blame her. I now had the answers I sought, yet nothing had really changed. She frowned, seemingly understanding my sentiment, but before bringing up something else that didn't quite make sense. "Wait a second. The last time I was in town, I'd heard Alison say that there was a wax figure that went missing many years ago. Was that Fred? And if it was, where did Ted come from?"

Oh, I can answer that.

"The damaged Fred was returned to the museum, where he remains in storage."

I hate when she does that—she always has to be first.

Regina looked slowly around the storage room, causing us to do the same. An uneasy feeling settled over me, and for the first time, I truly believed in the afterlife. Just what had been on this piece of land before the wax museum?

You really don't want to know the answer to that question. Let's save that for another day, shall we?

"Fred is probably in this very room somewhere."

"Then it's Ted who is missing," Heidi guessed, obviously as confused as I was as to how that could be. "Why has no one noticed the resemblance?"

Ted didn't resemble anyone famous, and he was able to walk around town without question. So just where had Ted come from?

Oh, Ted is from the wax museum, alright.

"Miss Rosemary made it so no one would recognize me."

Ted smiled, displaying a few broken teeth. It all began to come together...his height, his blondish white hair, his sunken eyes, the suit. I'd said it before, but I'd never imagined in a million years for it to be true.

Lurch.

"Ted Cassidy," Heidi and I both said in unison. Our Ted was a bit different, but the similarities were there all the same. "The Addam's Family."

Bingo.

Ted Cassidy had been a brilliant actor who'd played Lurch in "The Addam's Family" in the 1960s. He most likely would never have believed his wax figure would end up a henchman to a bona fide witch, but that was a legacy all unto itself, wasn't it?

"I guess I never gave it any thought," Regina said, tilting

her head as she gave Ted a once-over. Her lips pulled back in what appeared to be approval. "I can see the resemblance."

Why does she always have to—

I stepped forward and picked up Leo, whose left eye looked about ready to pop out. It was rare that we showed each other affection like he and Heidi did to one another, but I was feeling a bit sentimental. I hugged him to me and buried my face in his fur.

To Leo's credit, he put up with my need for comfort.

I wasn't the only one with family issues. We were his family, and he'd put up with our inner circle fighting for a very long time.

Does this mean I get extra catnip tonight?

"...don't believe they left the building. Someone would have seen—" Liam stopped in his tracks, taking in the scene before him. Jack wasn't far behind. The two handsome men stared at us in disbelief, but I wasn't quite sure how we were going to get out of this tiny predicament. Usually, Heidi was the quick-thinking one, but one glance revealed her lips opening and closing like a fish. "Raven? What's going on in here? We've been looking everywhere for you."

"If you're going to be dating my daughter, then you should know right now that she's not the world's most graceful woman," Regina exclaimed, succeeding in embarrassing me more than when she'd threatened to follow me and my date to prom my senior year of high school. "Don't worry. Raven is fine now that Ted picked her up off the floor."

Well, she just shined you off in a rather dull light, didn't she? I'm beginning to remember why we don't have her come visit more often.

I'm pretty sure Liam didn't buy what my mother was selling, either.

"Ted decided to come to the party, after all." I would stick as close to the truth as possible. I handed Leo to Ted, who physically showed his displeasure, but we all needed to act normal for the next few minutes. "And he refused to leave Leo behind. Wasn't that sweet of him?"

Put me down. Put me down right this minute. Put me down.

"Ted, would you care to keep me company while we ring in the New Year?" Regina asked, not really giving Ted a chance to say no...or Leo, for that matter. Ted fell into step beside my mother and the three of them left the storage room. "You know, Ted, there could be worse places to be than..."

Help! Help!

Leo wouldn't be able to physically disappear in front of so many guests, and he was well aware of that fact. I would probably pay with another vase or two in my near future, but it was worth it if it meant the town saw us as any other normal family.

"There's no blood," Heidi chimed in with a bright smile. "You should have seen her go down. My fault...totally. I couldn't resist taking more pictures with some of these wax figures in storage. I mean, can you believe they don't have Marilyn Monroe on display? And we found Jesse James in the back over there by the door. I'll admit that we opened that exit in the back to see if they had anyone else hidden who we might want to get a picture with, but there was no..."

Heidi led Jack out the door with her nonstop fabricated account of what had transpired in the last thirty minutes or so. Truthfully, I had no idea how much time had passed since Heidi and I had finally located Norman Palmer's wallet...which was still clutched in my hand.

Liam's dark gaze wasn't on the billfold or photograph in my hand.

"I came back this way, but you weren't in here," Liam said

as he clearly struggled with the story my mother and Heidi had cooked up. Technically, I did fall. And we did go searching the room for other wax figures. He surprised me by reaching out and brushing his thumb against my cheek. "You have a smudge of dirt. Are you sure you're okay?"

"Yes," I replied, unable to prevent my smile. I should be attempting to convince him that everything had happened the way it had been explained, but a warmth had spread through my entire body. I put my hands behind my back to hide the contents so this moment wasn't ruined. "I'm more than okay."

And I was also okay with how this mystery had unfolded.

Thinking over the events of this past weekend had me coming to one major conclusion—family mattered more than anything else. Family meant *all* those a person held dear to him or her.

My mother and grandmother might have been estranged by the end of Nan's life, but she'd clearly never given up that her granddaughter would return to continue the family legacy. Mom's regret of not letting bygones be bygones was evident, and Nan had done what she could to right a wrong—she'd given life to Ted, who had been her friend and confidant. She'd gotten the town to accept him as a distant relative of the Marigolds, and ensure that he could live for...

Wow.

Was Ted immortal?

Once again, another mystery for another time.

"It's almost midnight," Liam said quietly, still searching my gaze for answers I couldn't give...at least, not right now. I waited for Leo to make some sort of quip, but he must still be with Ted and my mother. "I'm sorry you didn't get the answers you were searching for in your research. I know that you wanted to clear any chance of doubt hanging over Rosemary's head concerning her involvement."

"I'm okay with not having all the answers," I replied carefully, not wanting to ever lie to Liam. I didn't have all the details of that fateful night. That much was true. Only Leo was still alive to tell the tale, and as we know...his memory wasn't the best. "I truly appreciate you letting me look at the case files. I can give them back to you when you take me home tonight."

"I have no worries about those old files. I'm sure you'll give them back to me when you're satisfied." Liam held up his palm for me to take with my hand. Now, didn't that sweet gesture put me in some type of conundrum? "Shall we? I'm sure it's getting close to midnight."

Sure enough, a round of cheers could be heard from the other room before a countdown began from ten. Liam glanced over his shoulder, giving me time to toss Norman Palmer's wallet over Marilyn Monroe's head. The soft thud as the billfold landed on a box somewhere was covered up by the shouting guests.

"Just in time," I replied, eagerly sliding my hand onto his. "Let's ring in this New Year and start it off right."

Liam led the way, closing the door behind on a mystery that he would never be able to claim as solved. I guess it wasn't so bad for the sheriff's department to have a slight blemish on their record. After all, no one was perfect.

"Five!"

Liam continued to weave in and out of the various guests staring up at the disco ball that Alison and Oliver Bend had so graciously crafted for this special occasion. Old traditions had become new, and the Marigolds were once again a part of the town's future.

"Four!"

We finally reached our destination next to our friends and family. Heidi and Jack were smiling as they watched the ball begin to descend from the ceiling. Otis and his wife were laughing at the confetti being dropped from the baskets above us. My mother was saying something to Ted, who stood next to her with Leo in his arms.

"Three!"

Granted, Leo looked a little worse for wear, but we were all together.

A family of witches, humans, a golem, and a ragtag familiar.

Is there a reason you put me last? I should be first on that list.

"Two!"

I hadn't been able to cast the enchantment I'd wanted to for Leo in hopes of restoring some of his memory, but I'd come to the conclusion that he was perfect just the way he was. In the end, everything always seemed to come together.

I have my work cut out for me, don't I?

"One!"

I'll admit, I was expecting a kiss.

"Happy New Year, Raven."

What I received was much more than that.

Liam twirled me toward him as the ball finally reached the end of the pole, confetti fluttering down upon us from above. His warm lips touched mine, and the most magical moment of my life had just been recorded in my mind. Usually, it was the first sip of coffee in the morning that curled my toes. Well, Liam's stimulating kiss might just top my first cup of sanity.

I finally opened my eyes after he pulled away, the cheers resounding throughout the building. A new year had been rung in, and I couldn't wait to see what surprises were in store for us.

"Happy New Year, everyone!"

You get the hunky sheriff, and I get...Ted? Not fair, Raven. Not fair at all.

~ The End ~

Ghostly antics and magical chaos turn into a hauntingly mischievous tale in this delightful continuation of USA Today Bestselling Author Kennedy Layne's cozy paranormal mystery series...

The small coastal Connecticut town of Paramour Bay has brought a lot of surprises to Raven Marigold's life, but she never expected to encounter a bona fide honest-to-gosh ghost!

It appears that Raven and her familiar have made quite the name for themselves on the other side as amateur sleuths... enticing an endearing tea-drinking spirit to seek their help to solve a kidnapping, of sorts. You see, the sweet apparition's familiar didn't follow her into the afterlife and has gone missing—even from the eyes of the dead!

Grab a cup of hot tea and a cozy blanket so that you can snuggle in front of the warm hearth of your fireplace with this riveting supernatural tale that will have you smiling well into the night!

Other Series By Kennedy Layne

Detective Kinsley Aspen Novels

Touch of Evil Series

The Graveside Mysteries

The Widow Taker Trilogy

Paramour Bay Mysteries

Hex on Me Mysteries

The Safeguard Series

Keys to Love Series

Office Roulette Trilogy

Surviving Ashes Series

Red Starr Series

CSA Case Files

About the Author

Kennedy Layne, a USA Today bestselling author, resides in the Midwest with her retired Marine Master Sergeant husband and their menagerie of pets. Fueled by coffee and her love for thrillers, cozy mysteries, and romantic suspense novels, Kennedy loves to spend time in front of her fireplace crafting stories that keep her readers guessing until the very end.

Email:
kennedylayneauthor@gmail.com

Website:
www.kennedylayne.com

Newsletter:
www.kennedylayne.com/newsletter.html

www.ingramcontent.com/pod-product-compliance
Lightning Source LLC
Chambersburg PA
CBHW060439180626
46817CB00007B/2893